Shoes for Daniel

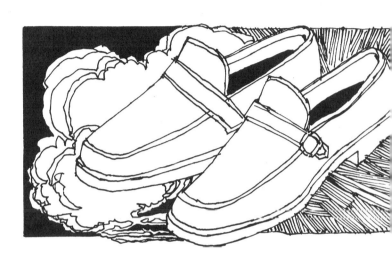

Shoes
for
Daniel

By Ernie Holyer

Southern Publishing Association
Nashville, Tennessee

This book was
Edited by Gerald Wheeler
Designed by Dean Tucker

Cover painting by
Buford Winfrey

Text set 12/14 Fairfield
Printed on Supple Antique
90% Recycled Paper
Cover stock: Carolina C1S

Printed in U.S.A.

Dedicated

to Dr. Norman E. Shumway

Spanish/English Translation

abuelo, abuelito .... grandfather
bracero .... laborer
buenas noches .... good-night
bueno .... good
buenos días .... good-day
Chicano .... name Spanish-Americans
call themselves
de la raza .... of the race (Mexican)
del río .... of the river
gato .... cat
gracias .... thanks
hombre .... man
la casa grande .... the big house
masa .... dough
muchas gracias .... many thanks
niños .... children
señor .... sir, Mr.
señora .... madam, Mrs.
sí .... yes

Contents

Leaving the Fields

Daniel Morales huddled low in the dusty red pickup truck as the cold morning air rushed through the broken side window. The boy's face felt like a stiff mask, and his ears burned under the flying strands of black hair. An occasional raindrop came hurtling through the window and slapped him in the face.

Papa's rickety old pickup truck roared toward San Jose, California. The Morales family and all their belongings bounced along in it. Papa, Daniel, Linda, and Angelina sat up front. Mamma lay on a mattress in the back of the pickup, covered by several yards of flapping canvas. She shared her bed with a camp stove, pots and pans, food, and empty fruit crates.

Signs zipped past. Daniel read them until the letters began to blur together: "Fresh berries." "Dried prunes and apricots." "Walnuts." The fruit stands changed their signs with the crops that came in.

Sunlight broke through the rain clouds. It shimmered on green hills and glanced off puddles left by the spring rains.

"Look, Angelina, a rainbow!" Linda cried, pointing toward the sky.

Angelina happily clapped her chubby little hands.

11

Daniel, however, felt no gladness. The broken arc in the sky made a sorry rainbow.

Orchards, pastures, and plowed fields vanished as farmland yielded to houses and gas stations. Señor Morales slowed the truck and intently watched the roadside. He passed several gas stations before pulling into one and parking by the washrooms.

The station attendant was busy washing windshields and pumping gas. Papa waited until the last car rolled out of the station. His face tight as leather stretched over a drum, he jumped from the pickup. Daniel held his breath. It was the first time his father had ever asked for a job that had nothing to do with field work.

Papa took his wide-brimmed hat off and held it in his hands. "Buenos días, señor."

"What do you want?" The attendant locked the cashbox and stuffed the key in his pocket.

"If it would please señor to give me a job," Daniel's father said, bowing low. "We need money. The wife, she got sick. We cannot follow the crops no more. She needs a place to rest."

The gas station man eyed him suspiciously. "Have you worked in a gas station before?"

"No, señor."

"Can you read English?" The attendant shoved a credit card under papa's nose.

Daniel's father read it, stumbling over each word and trying again.

The white man's face reddened with anger. "You Mexicans are all alike," he muttered. "You come in here and ask for jobs you know nothing about. Go and stick to picking fruit."

"Sí, señor, gracias."

As papa shuffled to the pickup, Daniel cringed inside. His father was a good mechanic. He kept the pickup running, didn't he? At self-service stations, he always filled the tank himself. If only the attendant knew what a good worker papa was! Papa could carry a full crate to the end of a row and still smile. But he was not smiling now.

Daniel remembered times when the row boss shouted, "Hey, you guys, you gotta *move!*" But no matter how much Señor Morales worked, somebody always yelled. The boy felt sorry for his father because the attendant had hurt his pride.

When papa hoisted himself back into the truck, Daniel looked the other way. The boy realized that a man does not want to be humiliated in front of his twelve-year-old son.

Daniel's father stopped at many more gas stations. They had no jobs for him. Each time his broad shoulders slumped a little more.

The north wind chased the clouds to the ridges of the Coast Range. The sun rode across the sky. Papa drove past new houses and neatly trimmed lawns. Every so often he stuck his head out of the window and looked for the vanished orchards he had once worked in.

"At one time the Santa Clara Valley was the prune bowl of the world," he addressed the children in Spanish. "We used to come here every year and pick prunes. Remember?"

"Sí, Papa. I remember." Daniel nodded.

Angelina bounced on Linda's knees. Linda was too busy to answer and did not turn to glance outside.

Papa craned his neck. "There are houses where orchards used to be, and what's left is up for sale." He stabbed a calloused hand at a red FOR SALE sign nailed against a fence post. Behind the fence lay rows of dying trees.

"There's no stopping it now," Daniel's father continued. "The subdividers buy, and the bulldozers rip out the trees. The good soil, it's going to be paved over."

A red traffic light gleamed ahead, and papa slammed on the brakes. He frowned at the bumper-to-bumper traffic.

"Cars and factories and foul air are in the cities," he grumbled. "They call it progress, and they're proud of it. What's worse, every year they make more mechanical harvesters. Pretty soon they won't need the bracero anymore."

Daniel sensed his father's anger. He thought of countless past mornings. At the crack of dawn they had trudged through a muddy field, following the pace-setting truck. The field bosses allowed no lagging behind, no stopping until the pickers had finished the row.

The family spent the nights in a labor camp. The roofs often leaked. It was almost as bad as sleeping in the pickup. After a breakfast of beans, they endured a cold ride to the field. By working hard and getting ahead of the truck, Daniel sometimes could rest a little until the vehicle caught up. But mamma—she fell behind. And then she could work no more. His mother had been slow ever since the family returned from their winter stay in Arizona. Now they were in California. Their relatives' place was a long way off.

Riding back to the camp the previous evening, Daniel had looked down from the cab of the pickup at the people in their warm cars. He had worried about mamma and what would become of the family. Though the grower's wife had paid papa off (the family had worked for weeks), they had little money to show for it.

Realizing that they couldn't keep on working in the fields, papa had headed north on the freeway. Daniel could see why he chose San Jose. Gas stations sprawled at every corner. One of them would surely give him a job.

The four-lane expressway papa had entered a while back funneled into a narrow road. "Why are we leaving the city, Papa?" Daniel fretted.

"We must find a cheap place to stay, Daniel," papa replied solemnly, looking straight ahead. Daniel missed his father's smile.

A pretty valley unfolded between the scalloped fringe of hills. Tree-studded hillsides tilted toward the sun. The growers had already plowed in the bright yellow mustard weeds. Whitewashed tree trunks stuck up like broomsticks, the branches sending out clusters of soft green leaves. Woolly-looking apricots nestled near the tips of the branches.

"Will we have a good 'cot year?" Daniel asked his father.

"I hope so, Daniel. You can earn some money cutting 'cots."

"Sí, Papa." Daniel leaned back and watched the countryside slide past. Redwing blackbirds whirred out of roadside ditches. Poppies splashed golden patches beside the road. A meadowlark trailed musical notes behind it as it swept past the pickup.

Prune blossoms sailed across the road, propelled by the wind. Sticking his hand out the window, Daniel managed to catch a bit of white fluff for his baby sister, Angelina, who sniffed it with delight. After floating like tiny parachutes, the blossoms landed on the valley floor.

Farmhouses peeked out between the flowers and

shrubs. Sedum made golden ribbons along a walk. Bottlebrush blushed along a wall. Barnyards reverberated with rooster crows. Bare walnut trees and grapevines flashed by.

Linda grinned. "The grapes and walnuts will need no harvesters for some long time," she remarked. At ten, the girl still did not understand that picking crops was the family's livelihood.

The hills ran together, and the pickup, clattering into a winding canyon, came to a town dozing between the shrubs and trees. Papa stopped at the town's entrance and peered at a marker on the right side of the road. "Can you read what it says, Daniel?"

"I will try, Papa." The boy studied the marker. " 'NEW ALMADEN,' " he read slowly. " 'Site of first mining operations in California. Mining began here in 1824. In constant production since 1845. Over one million flasks of quicksilver valued in excess of fifty million dollars have been recorded.' "

Señor Morales pushed back his hat. "It says all that?"

"Sí, Papa." Daniel was proud of his ability to read.

Daniel's father drove to the end of the settlement and at a narrow bridge made a sharp left turn, pulled around a house marked "Café del Río," and entered a side street. "Watch for signs," he instructed the children.

"What kind?" Daniel wanted to know.

"For sale, or for rent."

"Are we going to buy a house?" Linda gasped.

"No, Linda," papa said patiently. "Sometimes people rent if they cannot sell. Renting is better than letting a house stand empty." He shifted to a lower gear as the truck began to lug and buck.

Dogs chased and barked at the pickup as it dodged the mailboxes jutting into the road. Brush, fences, and corrals ran up the hill on Daniel's side. Weathered roofs ducked underneath the spreading crowns of oaks, sycamores, and pines. On papa's side, the hill fell off to a flowing creek.

Papa hit the brakes. "There's a sign!"

Daniel whipped around. "Where?"

The badly weathered FOR SALE sign leaned toward the ground. Behind the sign, a many-trunked bay tree dwarfed the house. From the distance of the street the building looked like a toy house.

Papa parked in the leaf-littered yard and checked on his wife. Putting his finger to his mouth, he whispered to the others, "Mamma fell asleep. We must not wake her." Walking to the house, he peered through the dusty windows. "It is a big house," he declared. "A kitchen and three rooms."

Daniel dashed down to the creek, Linda and Angelina following behind. A tangle of berry bushes covered the bank. "Look out for thorns!" Daniel warned his sisters. The creek gurgled like a well-fed baby. Silvery ripples glistened where the water danced and leaped over rocks. Lush watercress crept along the banks, its round leaves bobbing like miniature cradles. Daniel hoped they could rent the house. Surely it would make mamma well.

Returning to the pickup, papa slowly copied the phone number from the sign. Then he drove back down the road and parked near some picnic benches behind the restaurant. "Take good care of mamma and your sisters," he instructed Daniel. "I must find the people who want to sell the house."

"Sí, Papa." Daniel jumped from the cab of the

pickup and ran around to the back to check his mother. She was awake, her moon-shaped face sallow-looking, but her breath no longer came in gasps. Daniel helped her climb over the tailgate. "Sit on a bench, Mamma," he said. "Papa will come back soon."

Food smells drifted from the restaurant. Remembering the beans they carried along for lunches in the field, he located the pot in the back of the truck. "Eat, Mamma. You will feel better with food in your stomach." He set the bean pot on the picnic table, and Angelina crawled into her mother's lap. Linda brought spoons. As they ate, they brushed away the flies that came buzzing around. Daniel put the pot away before the bottom showed. "We must leave something for papa," he told the older sister, who still looked hungry.

"The beans made me thirsty," Linda complained.

"I will bring water," the boy replied, grabbing a pail and heading for the creek flowing behind the restaurant. As he slid down the steep bank, the thorny canes growing along it caught on his jeans and scratched his bare feet. Scum and dead branches floated on the stagnant water. Litter had choked the flow of the creek, and strong odors hung over the dirty water like a heavy cloak. Flies buzzed over the green algae scum. His pail still empty, he crawled back up the bank.

"We cannot drink this water," Daniel answered his sister's questioning look. "It will make us sick. I will search somewhere else."

Behind the restaurant Daniel found a dripping water faucet. He filled the pail and hurried back to his mother and sisters. First he offered the water to his mother. "Drink, Mamma. This is good water." They drank and waited while his father hunted for the people who owned the house. Cars hummed past on the road, and the shade shifted from one side of the building to another.

Automobiles pulled into the parking lot by the street. Car doors slammed behind them. Laughter rang out as the seemingly carefree people headed for the restaurant.

Would there be leftovers? Daniel wondered. Long ago he had learned to his amazement that some people left food on their plates. And would the cook throw the leftovers into the garbage cans beside the faucet? Daniel hoped so. The beans no longer quieted his stomach.

Wilted like a brown leaf, mamma could not cook the evening meal. The afternoon shadows grew long and skinny, and the spring evening wind started to bite. Shuddering in his thin T-shirt, Daniel helped his mother over the tailgate and into the shelter of the truck. The canvas and blankets inside it would keep her warm. After tucking her in, he joined his sisters in the cab. "I hope papa finds the people who rent the house," he told Linda.

"Do you suppose something happened to him? Mamma is sick, and we have no money." Linda clutched a sleepy Angelina and looked scared.

Her brother thrust out his chin. "Don't worry, Linda. I'll take care of the family if papa doesn't come back."

The sun slipped over the hill, and the night shadows crept into the trees. Where was papa?

Hunting for a Job

While the sun's red sheen faded from the sky, Linda dozed with Angelina on her lap. At last footsteps crunched on the gravel. "We did not get the house by the creek, Daniel," Señor Morales announced wearily, "but we have a place to stay." He boosted his stocky frame into the cab. Within seconds they arrived at a cabin off Main Street, the truck wheels splattering on the muddy drive.

"This is the house," papa said, jumping out. He pulled back the canvas flap and helped his wife over the tailgate. Linda carried a drowsy Angelina to the house and waited by the door. Daniel followed with the dew-dampened blankets and pillows. His father hoisted the mattress on his back and lugged it into a dark room. Shoved against a corner, it made a good enough bed.

Mamma hugged the children. "Buenas noches, niños. Pray and thank God for the good roof over our heads."

"Buenas noches, Mamma."

The family had slept in the crowded pickup many a night. Now Daniel missed the canvas roof and the feel of cold steel at his elbows as he listened to the strange noises in the yard. For once his bones did not ache from exhaustion. Not having to work in the field, tomorrow they could sleep as long as they pleased. Breathing poorly, mamma slept propped up on two pillows. How long, Daniel wondered, until she could work again? Worry nibbled away at his thoughts until he dozed off into a fitful sleep.

The next morning the sound of three or four barking dogs awakened him. Gray light filtered through the dull windowpanes, revealing that the room was a mess. Dust, cobwebs, and litter lay everywhere. Daniel slid from the mattress and stood up. A dirty sink, gas stove, and refrigerator showed through a doorway. The faucet gave no water. No gas hissed out of the burners when he turned them on, and the refrigerator yielded only musty odors. Exploring off the kitchen, Daniel stumbled into a closed-in porch and a dirty bathroom. A door, its paint peeling, led to the yard.

Daniel carried the camp stove in from the pickup. Returning for pots and pans, he suddenly stopped. Strange noises overhead caught his attention.

Loud, scolding sounds came from a live oak looming over the cabin. His flesh crawling, Daniel looked for their source. A gray animal leaped from branch to branch high in the tree. Daniel stepped closer to see better. The creature rushed to a limb above the boy, stamping its paws and jerking its tail in anger.

"A squirrel!" Daniel gasped in surprise. It was a full two feet long, its tail alone measuring a foot. The tree squirrel was much larger than the ground squirrels Daniel had watched on summer-dry hillsides.

"Do not scold like an angry woman," the boy told the animal. "I will not hurt you." He lifted the crate containing pots and pans from the pickup and carried it into the kitchen.

Papa, also up, lugged the bean and flour sacks into the house. Not having eaten since yesterday's breakfast, he was starved.

A few minutes later, Linda entered the kitchen, her long black hair parted near the top of her head. Tangles of it fell over her sweat shirt. "Mamma did not sleep well," she told her father.

"We must let her rest, Linda. You can cook, no?"

"Sí, Papa." Turning to her brother, she asked, "Can you bring water for the masa?"

"Sí, Linda." He dashed outside and found a rusty can filled with rainwater underneath the gutter spout. The water looked clean enough.

The girl began making the masa. First she mixed water and flour together and worked them into a lump. Sprinkling it with flour, she slapped the lump onto a pastry board. Then, pinching pieces from the lump, she shaped them into balls. The balls she rolled flat like pancakes. Daniel threw the disks onto the griddle and fried them on both sides.

"Eat the first ones, Papa," Daniel offered.

"Sí. I must be off," Señor Morales replied, gulping down the dry tortillas. Daniel guessed that his sister's cooking was not too good, but papa would not hurt Linda by mentioning it.

After his father drove away in the rattling pickup to find a job, Daniel stacked the tortillas in a kettle and covered it with a towel. "We should have cooked beans last night," he told his sister. "Now we have no filling."

Linda licked her lips. "If we had good filling and cornhusks, we could make tamales."

"I will cook some, Linda. We must give papa a good meal when he comes home." Daniel bustled about the camp stove, preparing a pot of beans. A grin spread over Linda's face.

"Papa did not eat the beans we saved for him yesterday, Daniel. We can eat them now." She got the beans from the pickup, refried them, and rolled them into the tortillas. With fresh beans cooking on the camp stove, the brother and sister carried the meager breakfast to their mother. Sitting on the mattress together, they ate the tortillas.

Daniel's heart ached for his mother. She never complained about her hard life. Her songs and laughter had cheered Daniel when he was a little boy. Since Angelina's birth some two years ago, mamma had not laughed much, and she never sang anymore.

After breakfast Angelina stayed with mamma while Daniel swept the cabin and Linda arranged fruit crates for furniture. Fruit crates always came in handy. Compared to the shelters some growers had provided, the cabin was a fine place indeed. It had no open slats, but solid walls and real windows. Since papa had paid the rent, they could call it their home for a whole month.

About to sweep the litter through the porch door, Daniel noticed a squirrel on a brush pile. Its busy claws rustled the dry twigs and branches. Daniel kept on sweeping. The squirrel froze, studied the boy a moment, then scampered up a tree trunk. Halting on a branch, it fluffed its bushy tail and gazed down. Daniel put away the broom and chuckled. "The cabin is clean," he told Linda. "I will go and hunt for a job."

"All by yourself?" Linda almost dropped the kettle she was holding. "You are very brave, Daniel."

"Watch over mamma and the baby. I will be back." He marched down the street, trying to appear braver than he felt inside. Cars swished past him with terrifying speed. In the town's twenty-five-mile-an-hour zone, they went more like fifty.

A police car zoomed past Daniel, its yellow lights flashing like the eyes of a mountain lion. The officer pulled a speeder over to the shoulder and got out to ticket him. The boy walked around the police car. The feel of his feet on crushed rock beside the pavement made him homesick for the soft soil of the fields.

Hammer blows and the whine of a Skilsaw sounded overhead. Somebody was building a house on the hillside high above the road. Its frame showed between the trees. Carpenters and bricklayers worked around the new house. One man pounded nails into rafters. Another sawed off overhanging boards. Two more men constructed a fireplace. Daniel wondered how and where men learned such useful trades. Construction workers drove better pickups than his father did. They made good money.

He climbed the winding road to the construction site and stopped beside a lumber stack. Much scrap wood littered the ground. The carpenter on the roof switched off his Skilsaw. "Want somethin', boy?"

"Sí, uh—do you have a job for me, señor? I could clean up scrap so you don't fall over it."

"Fall over it? Not a chance!" The man laughed.

"I could hand boards up to you." Daniel wrested a board from the stack.

"Never mind, boy. You're too young for this kind of work. How old are you anyway? Ten?"

"I am twelve years old, señor." His face reddened with embarrassment. He did not like to be reminded that he was shorter than non-Chicano boys his age.

"We hire no kids around here, boy. Better get out of the way before you get hurt." The carpenter switched on his Skilsaw and paid no more attention to the boy. Disappointed, Daniel plodded back down the hill.

At the edge of town he walked along a pasture fence. Half-grown cattle grazed side by side, their brown tails flicking about. Their yellow teeth ground together as they clipped off blades of grass.

"Come here, you fat little fellow," Daniel called, reaching through the barbed wire to touch the white-faced animal nearest him. It jumped and bounded off. The other cattle ran after it to the creek.

"I scared them away." Daniel slapped his forehead and hoped nobody noticed what he had done. Non-Chicanos always scolded him for whatever he did.

A whitewashed picket fence rambled along a drive-way and over a little bridge to several sprawling farm buildings. Daniel followed the driveway to where a man in coveralls stood washing a car. The boy stopped a distance from the man and waited until he noticed him. "What do you want, boy?"

"A job, señor. I can pick berries." Daniel's mouth felt dry.

"Haven't got any berries, just walnuts. Sorry." The man continued washing the car.

"Gracias, señor." Daniel trudged back to the road. Out in the valley he attempted to stop at three farm-houses to see if they had a job for him. At the first house, a fierce mongrel yapped at Daniel. A huge Labrador rushed to the gate of the second yard. And at the third house a grouchy old man scared Daniel off.

Going to the other side of the road, he retraced his steps. The canyon wall rose to Daniel's right. Poison oak and saplings grew in crevices in the rock. He steered clear of the poison oak and brushed aside overhanging tree branches. He walked to the town's upper end without finding another grower to ask for a job.

A firehouse perched on a hill, voices blaring from a loudspeaker system mounted under the eaves. The fire truck stood in a whitewashed barn down by the street, ready for an emergency. The bridge papa had crossed the day before stood near the fire station. Daniel remembered the historical marker he had seen then and looked for it.

"Site of first mining operations in California," he read again. "Here in Alamitos Creek in 1824 Luis Chabolla and Antonio Sunol first worked New Almaden ore in an arrastra and sluice."

Alamitos Creek. Creek of the little cottonwoods. Daniel liked the name. And the bridge over the creek intrigued him. He wondered whether the creek dried up in the summer like other California streams. Its babbling voice invited Daniel to come and see it. He slid down the embankment to where the water gurgled busily as it flowed along. Foam spilled over the rocks littering the creek bed. Daniel sat on a boulder and watched the current hurl twigs and leaves along. One could dream under the willows and tules. Here he could pretend his mother was well. Fragrant peppermint grew all around him. Plucking a leaf, he crushed it and sniffed. Sycamores and eucalypti nodded overhead. What a fine place! he told himself. Water, shade, everything. He wished he could stay forever—not have to return to the hot, dusty fields.

Cars rolled over the bridge and crunched to a halt on the gravel of a wide parking area above the creek. What were they doing? He scrambled up to the triangular area between the highway, the side road, and the restaurant. It sparkled with cars like a many-colored jewel. People from the cars crossed the street and headed for the brown-shingled church behind a row of giant eucalyptus trees.

Feeling trapped, Daniel waited until the people entered the church. When not even a child remained on the church steps, he scooted across the gravel and ran down the side road. Atop the first hill, he slowed and looked back over his shoulder.

As long as he could remember, Daniel had watched the growers' children as he stooped over the warm soil. Dressed in fine clothes, wearing good shoes, they had left for school or for church. And always he had felt a knot in his stomach.

Shoes Are for Rich Kids

A terrier pup bounded to his feet. Forgetting the growers' children, Daniel bent over and scratched the pup's wiry head. A baby cried in the house on the hilly bend, while a woman hung diapers in the yard. She glanced in Daniel's direction. "Puppy, come here," she called.

"Woof!" The terrier glanced at her but did not want to leave.

"Go on home," Daniel urged.

"Woof!" The pup trotted away.

A path angled down to the creek. Following it, he reminded himself that he should hunt for work; then decided he could do that later. The path led through a thicket of oaks and sycamores. Blue jays streaked blue and white through the branches and screeched a welcome.

Winter floods had piled up a gravel bank in the creek. Daniel curled his toes around the smooth pebbles. Choosing a flat boulder for a seat, he watched the watercress bob in the space between the rocks. Long-legged insects flicked about on the surface of the crystal-clear water like toy helicopters, casting huge shadow patterns on the algae-covered rocks below. Monarch butterflies bumbled on the flowering plants downstream. Their orange and black wings reminded him of the Halloween candy the growers sometimes gave to the bracero children.

Somebody had built a rock dam across the creek. Below the dam, tall stands of tule braced themselves against the tug of the current. Frothy ripples glistened in the sun where the water pooled behind rocks. Daniel walked across the sun-warmed rocks of the dam and chuckled to himself. The creek lifted the weariness and worry off his mind for a few moments.

Daniel had dreamed of such places as the creek. Often he had thought of exploring the countryside. But after a day's work, his bones had ached, and adventure no longer beckoned. Now, pausing a moment, he listened to the creek's gurgling song. It murmured a thousand and one beautiful secrets.

Suddenly, shouts jerked Daniel out of his daydreams. Several children had begun playing on the road uphill. He debated whether he should go back over the road or wade upstream. He hated to pass the happy youngsters lest they taunt him for being a Chicano, but, pressing his lips tightly together, he decided to take the road.

Four youngsters—two on each side of the road—threw a ball back and forth to one another. "Two, three, four!" they yelled, hurling the ball, leaping up to catch it. Daniel watched them a moment, wishing he could make friends with them. He wondered what it would be like to play with boys his age. Walking between them, he said, "Excuse me."

They kept on tossing the ball, not even noticing him. Daniel plodded home, feeling guilty because he had not earned any money all day.

The Morales' pickup stood in the yard, the four corner pipes on the truck bed sticking up like bedposts, the connecting bars naked. His father had removed the canvas. The hood gaped open, and papa sprawled over the engine.

"Buenos días, Papa."

"Buenos días, Daniel. Did you find work?"

"No, Papa. Did you?"

"No, Daniel," he answered, holding up a greasy metal object. "Instead of asking for jobs, I hunted from junkyard to junkyard to get this piece cheap. The pickup, she is like a spoiled woman. She goes only when she wants to." He looked annoyed.

"Poor papa!" Daniel thought. All his free time he spent fixing the pickup. The boy felt even more guilty for having loafed all day. The smell of cooking drifted from the kitchen. When his stomach growled, Daniel felt surprised that he should feel hungry. He had done no work all day. At the door of the house Angelina clasped the boy's legs while clutching a lollipop.

"Look, Daniel!"

"Who gave you this?" Daniel hoisted his sister into his arms.

"Papa." Angelina rocked back and forth. She wanted her brother to give her a fast ride in his arms.

Daniel raced the giggling girl around the cabin. Everybody spoiled Angelina. After the baby's birth, Mrs. Morales had been quite ill, and the family feared the tiny baby would not live. "Let us name her Angelina," mamma had suggested, "for soon she will be a little angel in heaven," she said, reflecting her Roman Catholic background. When Mrs. Morales recovered and the baby grew, the family showed their happiness by having Angelina's ears pierced for good luck. Papa himself had brought the child golden earrings.

Now Daniel kissed the golden dots and set the toddler down. "Go to mamma."

"Mamma!" Legs sprawled apart, Angelina waddled to the bed. Used to crawling between furrows, she had not walked much on smooth floors. Daniel was glad that for a change Angelina had a dry place to stay. His mother stroked several curly wisps of hair from Angelina's forehead as Daniel boosted the toddler onto the mattress.

Mamma grasped the boy's arm. "Where did you go, Daniel?"

"Not far, Mamma." Sitting on the edge of the bed, Daniel told her the day's happenings. He knew she would not scold. She never hollered at him. Like a sponge, she soaked up everybody's troubles and kept them within herself. Daniel always felt better after talking with her.

"You may find a job tomorrow, Daniel," she said, cradling her son's head between her gentle hands. "Even if you do not find a job, trust in God, Daniel. He is kind. He cares for us!"

"Sí, Mamma." Just as he turned toward the door, his father entered.

"The pickup, she is fixed," papa announced, a broad smile cheering his handsome face. The family gathered around mamma for the evening meal, then settled for the night.

Next morning papa started the pickup early and roared off like somebody who must make up for lost time. Daniel got water from the faucet behind the Café del Río. While there, he lifted the lid off one of the garbage cans and found half a loaf of bread and two rolls someone had thrown away.

After breakfast he walked out of the canyon. Despite barking dogs, he braved several farmhouses out in the valley, but with no luck. Nobody offered him a job.

Several abandoned farmhouses squatted among weeds and rambling shrubs. One day soon someone would tear them down to make room for new housing tracts. Many acres of neglected orchards and vineyards would suffer the same fate. Daniel felt sorry for the fruit trees and vines gone to waste.

In time the city would swallow everything. Then what would his father do? How would the family make a living? How would they eat? Dusty FOR SALE signs glared at Daniel. He did not want to see them.

How did mamma know that God really cared about what happened to them? Daniel wondered. He watched two hawks circling in the sky. Wings straight out, they sailed on the air currents. Daniel wished he could fly. Seen from so high above the ground, the world must look beautiful. From such great heights you could not see the ugly things. Litter, for example. Daniel kicked a beer can out of his way. Every now and then motorists threw a piece of trash out of their cars as they passed by.

Gazing at the hawks, Daniel thought that birds might be a little bit like God. Did God see the ugly things on earth? Poverty, hunger, sickness? Did God know his mother was sick? If heaven was far away, how could He see what took place on earth?

One hawk swooped down. Wings folded, he dived toward a pasture and snatched a field mouse. Amazed, Daniel watched the bird soar back into the sky. The hawk *had seen* the mouse from his lofty glide.

"Maybe God does see things on earth," Daniel said to himself. "He sees because His eyes are sharper than those of a hawk. God knows that mamma is sick and that papa needs a job. But does He *care?*"

Hoofbeats rang on the road as a girl rode up from the valley. Two black dogs trotted beside her black mount. Black horse, black dogs, black curls. He wondered who she was. Shade from the nearby oak trees hid her face, but he guessed she might be twelve, his own age.

"Hi!" the girl called in a friendly voice from the opposite side of the road.

"Hi!" Daniel pressed against the canyon wall as a passing truck nearly swept him off his feet. The girl galloped past, black curls bouncing on her shoulders, her boots hugging the horse's sides. Crossing the road, Daniel began walking in the horse's tracks, feeling good and light inside. A rich girl had greeted a Chicano boy! He knew she was rich because of her boots and saddle. Wondering if he would see her by the church sometime, he decided he would watch for her. The girl must be good, because she was kind to speak to a bracero boy.

Mamma said God was kind. But how did she know that He cared for poor people? "Make mamma well, dear God," he prayed. "If You make her healthy, I will know You are kind. I will know You care." The sun warmed him and soft breezes caressed his bare arms. A feeling of well-being rippled through him.

"God is good to us always," he scolded himself. "His sun warms us by day, and His breezes cool us by night. Both the rich and the poor enjoy the sun and the breezes. God *is* kind. He *does* care. And God *will* make mamma well."

Red lights flashing, a school bus hurtled past Daniel and screeched to a stop just in front of him. Its brakes hissed like air escaping from a huge tire. The children jumped off and scuffed the gravel with their shoes.

A boy and a girl entered Bertram Road, a side road which Daniel guessed was the same that started at the del Río restaurant. He followed them at a distance. They looked back once, then skipped over a bridge and disappeared around the bend.

Daniel leaned over the bridge's weathered railing. If he had shoes, he thought, he could go to church and perhaps see the kind girl again. With shoes, he could go to clean places like a school. As he listened to the creek, it seemed to murmur, "Shoes, shoes, shoes."

Daniel tried to swallow his disappointment. He would never own shoes; not until he was grown like his father. Shoes were for rich kids.

Alamitos Creek

Daniel left the bridge in no hurry to return home, for he would have to tell his father that he had not found a job. A chestnut colt whinnied at a nearby fence as if to ask Daniel to come closer. Since the colt had only cattle for company, Daniel guessed it was lonely.

Daniel stroked the colt's bristly mane and whispered, "Good boy."

A goat bleated from a fenced-in yard. Daniel left the colt and walked in the goat's direction. Tethered to the house, it stood on the porch, ears straight out.

"Baa! Baa!" it cried.

"Baa!" Daniel answered.

The goat hopped, and the brass bell around its neck sang a happy song. Daniel wished he could enter the yard and play with the little goat.

On Main Street an old man pulled a letter from a mailbox. The letter clamped under his arm, he leaned his weight on a walking stick and anxiously peered up and down the street. Obviously he wanted to cross over to Daniel's side of the road. Daniel slowed his steps, deciding to let him cross and get ahead of him. You never knew about people. They yelled every time they thought you were in the way or going too slow—especially if you were young or Chicano.

The man walked with jerky little steps. Cars screeched to a halt, and their drivers scowled at him. Suddenly the old man froze in the center of the street, a flustered expression on his pink face. Peering at the cars, he just stood there.

Then the boy noticed the man's hair. It was white as cotton. Only grandfathers had such white hair. A few leaps carried Daniel into the street. "Wait, abuelo! Let me help you!" Offering his arm, he guided the man to safety. A few drivers smiled, and the cars moved on.

"Thank you, young feller," the man said, his voice brisker than the rest of him.

"It was nothing, señor." The boy hurried off before the man asked any questions. He felt sorry for old people. When they had lived many seasons, their eyes grew dull and their limbs stiffened. Like the last leaves on the trees, they were bound to fall.

At home Daniel found his father back from San Jose, filling the house with his comfortable laugh. "Look at your papa, Daniel!" he said, tapping his chest. "Rolando Morales, he is now a gas station man."

"I am glad for you, Papa." All his life Daniel had seen his father harvesting crops in the fertile valleys of California, bending over the furrows, climbing fruit trees, lugging crates. It was hard to think of him as a gas station man. Papa was a good worker, though. He had to be, for if a bracero did not work hard, somebody else always waited to take his place. The gas station was lucky to get a hard worker like him.

"Get the hoe, Daniel," papa said importantly. "Today we will plant a crop."

"Sí, Papa," Daniel replied, bringing the tool.

Taking it, Señor Morales broke the soil in the yard's

sunniest spot. He had brought tomato and pepper plants from San Jose, which he planted with much ceremony while mamma, Linda, Angelina, and Daniel watched.

"When the plants get big, we will harvest our own tomatoes, no, Papa?" Daniel asked.

"Sí, Daniel, and peppers, too," papa said, firming the soil around the plants.

Then the whole family stood in a circle admiring the garden patch. The Morales family had become growers.

Señor Morales turned to his son. "The plants need water, Daniel."

"Sí, Papa." Grabbing the bucket near the porch door, he started to hurry away.

"Come back, Daniel!" Linda called. "We have water in the kitchen. The man from the water company turned it on."

"Is it true?" He dashed into the kitchen. A stream of water gushed from the faucet. Then he carried the full bucket to the garden patch, where his father poured the water into the trenches he had dug around the plants.

Looking rested, mamma went inside. As always, she worked as soon as she felt better, cooking rice for the evening meal and afterward cleaning the kitchen. In the morning, she rose with her husband.

"Linda and I must clean this place. The house is a mess," she persisted despite papa's protest.

After breakfast Daniel offered to help with the cleaning.

Mamma patted the boy's head. "Housework is not for men, Daniel. You have worked hard. Today you can do as you please."

"Gracias, Mamma." He dashed off to the creek.

Out on Bertram Road he met a boy beating a long

stick against a hedge. His hair glistening in the sun like corn silk, he looked about Linda's age.

"Hi!" Daniel greeted in passing.

The boy turned around and glanced at Daniel. He wore good shoes and new jeans. Offering no greeting, he went back to beating the hedge.

Daniel hung his head. Sometimes the growers' children had come to the field and asked him to play. But Daniel had kept on working with the family. He had had no time for playing or for making friends.

As Daniel turned into the path to the creek, blue jays welcomed him. Sun spots twinkled on the ripples. Noticing movements beneath the surface, he stooped over the water. A crayfish labored clumsily to get underneath a board. His rust-brown body showed green markings at the joints.

"You would not do as a fruit picker." The boy laughed.

At last the crayfish worked himself underneath the plank, only his antennae and pincer claws showing on the board's shady side.

"You are a smart one," Daniel said. "You like shady lookout spots."

The crayfish lay still, seemingly tired out from moving around. Daniel wondered how such a clumsy creature could survive. Then he noticed a number of gray objects darting about. Thumb-size fish flitted in the water. The tiniest ones chased each other around rocks. The larger fish hovered just below the surface of the creek. A big one snapped at some floating specks. Ever-widening ripples drifted across the water.

"I would like to be a fish," Daniel thought aloud. "Of all creatures, fish are the luckiest. They can swim and play and stay out of the hot sun."

38   SHOES FOR DANIEL

The tiny fish pursued each other to the plank where the crayfish lay. The crayfish's pincer claw jerked forward and caught the creature a meal. It happened so quickly that Daniel could hardly believe what he saw. He no longer envied fish, and no longer worried about the crayfish getting enough food. Nature had given the crayfish skill to survive.

"I would like to be a crayfish maybe," Daniel told himself. "All a crayfish does is wait for food. He never has to beg for a job." Sitting on a boulder and placing his feet on half-submerged rocks, Daniel watched spiders move as light as feathers over the dry pebbles along the creek shore, and seed heads tremble on tufts of grass. Stones and driftwood formed little islands in the creek. The breeze rippled the green sprouts of willow branches.

Something scuttled around his foot. He picked up a stick and, careful not to hurt whatever had moved, turned over the rock to reveal a reddish crayfish. A smaller gray one lay beside it. The small crayfish backed into the mud. The larger one clumsily turned and clambered up to the bank to stick out its antennae as if testing for danger. Daniel guessed it had not noticed him even though it dropped back into the water. Its right pincer claw was huge and lopsided from an accident. The crayfish crawled into the shade of a rock. It, too, liked smooth and shady places.

Air brakes hissed on the road as a school bus let off children. Daniel was glad his father did not make him go to school while the family lived at New Almaden. He remembered many unhappy days in different schoolhouses when he had to face new teachers and strange faces. Sometimes the children had laughed because Daniel did not speak good English. Other times he had not understood what the teacher said. He hoped the school people would leave him alone. Once summer vacation started, nobody cared anyway.

School buses drove up from the valley through New Almaden every day, the happy faces of children peering through the windows. Daniel wondered how they could possibly be happy about going to school. Lifting his chin, he decided he was content just to sit by the creek.

He hoped the family would leave town soon. His mother got up every day now. During the morning she cooked and cleaned and seemed impatient to move on. But by evening her legs swelled like balloons.

One day Señor Morales brought home his first paycheck. The family's hopes and future seemed to brighten. Then one morning mamma was extremely ill after sitting up all night, fighting for breath. By dawn her eyes protruded from dark circles. Daniel thought she must have seen frightening things like he did sometimes in his dreams.

Papa stayed with mamma all day. He wanted to call a doctor, but mamma asked him not to. "Doctors cost much money," she said. "I have been like this before. I will get better with rest."

The next day she did feel better, and papa drove to work. An hour later his pickup rattled back into the yard.

Daniel ran out to find out what was wrong. "Is there no work at the gas station today?" he asked.

"Sí, Daniel," papa replied, shutting off the motor. Tired creases wove cobwebs in his face.

"Then why are you back?"

"I am fired, Daniel."

"Why, Papa?"

"Because I did not work yesterday." He put a finger

to his mouth and glanced at the cabin.

"Mamma is sleeping, Papa. She cannot hear you." The boy lowered his voice. "What did the boss say?"

"The boss was angry, Daniel. He said, 'Why don't you Mexicans pull yourselves up by your bootstraps?'"

Daniel stared at his bare feet and wondered how a Chicano could pull himself up by the bootstraps when he has no boots. Aloud he said, "Did you not tell the boss that mamma was sick?"

"Sí, Daniel. I told him."

"But why did he fire you?" The boy did not understand.

"The boss is not de la raza, Daniel. He does not understand that Mexican people must stay with the family when something is wrong."

Surprised, Daniel asked, "Does the boss stay with his wife when she gets sick?"

"I guess not. People like this boss never miss a day's work."

"I am sorry you lost your job, Papa." He sensed the hurt behind his father's tired smile.

"Do not worry, my son. Your papa, he will find a new job tomorrow."

But Señor Morales did not find work tomorrow, nor the next day. Days passed, a week. Each morning he drove off to look for work, only to return unsuccessful that evening. The family's money dwindled; the landlord demanded another month's rent.

Daniel carried his worries to the creek. An hour by the gurgling water helped ease the day's troubles. Although he racked his brain for ways he could earn money, he could think of little to do besides work in the fields. Then an idea struck him. "Perhaps I can earn money minding babies!" He sprang to his feet. Several young couples lived on Bertram Road. They must have babies.

Diapers waved in the breeze at the house on the hilly bend. Daniel gathered up his courage to ask for a baby-sitting job. If his father could become a gas station attendant, he, Daniel, could become a baby-sitter.

The terrier pup yipped and jumped behind the screen door, wanting to come out and play. A woman appeared behind the screen and locked the door with a bang. "No, puppy, no!" she scolded. "Shame on you." Curlers covered the woman's head. Despite them, she was quite pretty.

Daniel did not bother to ask for a job, even though he had believed that beautiful women were supposed to be sweet and kind—and not scold. He plodded along Bertram, listening for a baby's cry.

Somebody was raking gravel in a yard, the scraping noises mixing with the screech of blue jays and the chatter of squirrels. From a high spot he watched a woman pushing a baby buggy toward the Café del Río. A poodle danced around her pale legs like a dark shadow. She picked up her pet and pushed the buggy while carrying the dog.

Passing them, Daniel peeked underneath the buggy's top. The small baby waved his tiny fists in front of its face, then smiled up at him. The infant's mother herself had a babylike face. Daniel smiled at them. To his amazement, the woman did not ignore him, but smiled back.

"You have a beautiful baby, señora," he said, feeling a bit bolder. "It must be a pleasure indeed to mind a baby such as this one."

"Why, thank you." Happy dimples showed in the mother's face.

"I know a sitter," he ventured. "A sitter who has much experience in handling babies."

"You do? I could use some help in the mornings." The woman struggled with the squirming poodle. "Who is this sitter?"

"It's, uh—my sister Linda," Daniel stuttered. "Linda knows all about babies." He did not know why he offered his sister instead of himself.

"Can you send her to my house tomorrow morning? I live uphill, the Henderson house." She pointed to it.

"Sí, señora, sí!"

He zoomed around the restaurant at the corner and dashed for home. Getting there, he gushed out his news. Linda grinned at it, fat sausages appearing under her gleaming brown eyes. She loved babies and had cared for her baby sister just like mamma herself. Angelina was the doll Linda never had.

Suddenly Daniel thought of something that worried him. "What if the Señora Henderson does not want you?"

His sister's grin vanished as quickly as it had appeared. Mamma answered in the girl's place. "When the señora sees Linda's smile, she will want her. Do not worry, Daniel. Everybody likes Linda when she smiles."

Daniel nodded. "This is true." People's frowns usually vanished when Linda smiled.

The next morning he escorted his sister to the Henderson house. Scrubbed clean, wearing her long hair tied behind her neck, Linda did not look like the girl he knew. When Daniel rang the doorbell, the poodle yipped at the window, standing on a chair like a stuffed toy. Mrs. Henderson answered the doorbell, her face falling at sight of the little girl.

If Daniel Had a Bike

"Is *this* your sister?" Mrs. Henderson asked, towering over the girl.

"Sí, señora." Daniel gripped Linda's arm so the girl could not run off.

Mrs. Henderson shook her head. "Why, she's only a little girl," she exclaimed. "I expected at least a teen-ager."

"Linda is a good baby-sitter, better than a teen-ager," Daniel defended his sister.

Mrs. Henderson faced Linda. "How old are you, honey?"

"Ten." When the girl's mouth began to tremble, her brother feared she might burst into tears.

Fortunately the baby screamed in the house, and Mrs. Henderson rushed inside. The screaming baby on her arm, she returned to say, "I'm afraid I can't use you, Linda. I'm sorry."

Daniel's sister did not seem to hear Mrs. Henderson. She heard and saw only the baby. "Oh, what a beautiful baby!" she exclaimed. "May I hold her, señora? I never saw such a pretty baby before." The corners of Linda's expressive mouth tilted up. A hint of a smile flickered around her somber chin.

44

"Don't drop her!" Mrs. Henderson said, placing the infant in her arms.

Linda fussed with the baby until it gurgled in contentment. "Hear, señorà? She quit crying." Then the girl handed the baby back to its mother with a big grin.

Having watched Linda every moment, the woman seemed pleased. "Come on in, Linda. You're hired," she said.

"Muchas gracias, señora!" She followed Mrs. Henderson into the house.

Linda took care of the Henderson's child five mornings a week. Every noon, she brought her father the dollar she had earned. Papa saved it, with the money he earned at a new gas station, for the landlord.

Only Señora Morales and Daniel contributed nothing to the family's income. Mamma cooked the meals but had to go to bed when her swollen legs could no longer support her weight. In Linda's absence, she watched over Angelina.

Daniel felt lost without work. The sadness in his mother's eyes drove him out of the cabin. Daily he went to the creek where the crayfish lay. The creek listened to Daniel's troubles and gave him a feeling of peace.

One morning Daniel ambled down to the creek, looking for ripe berries. They had sparkled like bits of red fire in the brambles along the creek bank for many weeks. To Daniel's horror, he discovered that a bulldozer had ripped out the bushes. Uprooted, they died on the slope. Rocks and dust showed under the wilted canes. The wind would blow the soil away, and after that nothing would grow on the naked rocks. Anger rose in Daniel.

"People always destroy things," he grumbled. "Papa says that nature covers the earth with living things.

Then man comes along and ruins everything. Why don't people have better sense?"

Once on his favorite rock, however, Daniel forgot about people and what they did. Insects hummed about him. A dragonfly hovered over the water, its wings shimmering with color. The drowsy voice of the creek lulled Daniel into pleasant daydreams.

The arrival of a panel truck across the creek jolted Daniel alert. The truck backed up toward the bank, and a burly man jumped out. He glowered at Daniel but did not scold him. Daniel stole quietly away. With people staring at him, the creek lost its magic.

Two squirrels chased each other over a Bertram Road fence. The playful creatures noticed Daniel and dashed off in different directions. Daniel chuckled to himself.

Dappled sunlight danced on several bicycles lying in a nearby yard. Their owners had thrown them in a heap. Daniel felt sorry for the bicycles. They deserved better treatment. The fenders of the two blue bikes looked dull and dented. A red bike showed rust-covered handlebars. If he, Daniel, should ever own a bike, he would take good care of it. But then he would never own anything as exciting as a bicycle.

He ripped a leaf from a bay tree, crushed it between his fingers, and sniffed. The pungent aroma rushed up his nose, shooting tears into his eyes, which he had to blink away. A bay leaf never failed to clear a fellow's head.

Patches of shade flickered on the pavement. Ants marched across them to a dead lizard in the road. The sight of the dead animal chilled the boy. He remembered times when he had envied the carefree little lizards as they scampered across the fields. He was glad to be alive; this helped him not to feel sorry for himself. "Even if I had a bike, I couldn't ride it in the fields," he reminded himself.

From the bridge, Daniel noticed a group of little blond-haired boys feeding ducks down by the water.

"Hi, there!" one called up to Daniel as he crossed the bridge.

"Hi!" Daniel stopped, wondering what the boy wanted.

"Who is that?" a second child asked.

Not wanting to hear what the boys might say about him, Daniel continued on down the road. At the corner of Main and Bertram a fluffy white cat leaped from a fence post and missed Daniel's shoulder. Its padded feet landed on the ground.

"Meow!" the cat cried.

"What do you want, gato?" Daniel chuckled.

"Meow!" The cat wrapped itself around the boy's leg, its amber eyes begging and its voice pleading.

"Go home, gato. I must not take you with me," he explained, stroking the animal. The cat seemed to understand. Bounding over the fence, it ran to the corner house. The porch was empty, the drapes drawn. Nobody was home.

"Poor gato," Daniel sympathized.

In the middle of the town Daniel spotted a driveway or narrow road between two ancient adobe buildings leading straight to his creekside boulder. Daniel studied the buildings. The first one, which had formerly served as post office, stood empty. The second building housed a museum. Clay pots hung out front and a poster showed an Indian tossing a piece of ore to a black-bearded miner. Daniel skirted the museum because of its bristling warning signs. The empty house, however, had a sign which declared, "PERMISSION TO PASS—REVOCABLE AT ANY TIME."

What did *revocable* mean? he wondered. If he took out the hard word, the sign said, "Permission to pass at any time." Maybe that's what it meant: you had permission to pass.

The driveway beckoned him on. He could cross the creek over the rock dam without so much as getting his feet wet. Unable to resist the shortcut, he dashed light-footed toward the creek.

"May I ask where you are going?" a woman's razor-sharp voice slashed the air behind him.

"I—uh, to the creek." He retraced his steps, glancing around to see where she was.

"You are not to go to my creek!"

Daniel saw that the woman stood beside the empty house. "You mean the creek—belongs to you?" he stammered.

"Yes, the creek is my property. We all own the creek." Middle-aged and heavyset, she charged at him like an angry turkey.

"I—uh, did not mean any harm." Daniel stared at his toes for a moment. Then, his face flushed, he plodded to the sidewalk. If only he had not left the street. If only he had stayed home. Why were people always bawling him out for things he didn't know anything about?

"I wonder if she would have chased me off if I were somebody important, somebody with money in his pocket?" Daniel muttered in anger. The woman reminded him of certain growers he had worked for. Many of them had everything you could possibly hope for, yet they would not give even the time of day to a lowly bracero.

"We all own the creek." Her voice echoed in Daniel's ear. Who was "we all"? Did it mean he no longer could visit the quiet spot where the crayfish lived? And did it mean he no longer could enjoy the creek?

Suddenly the full meaning of the woman's words dawned on him. From now on, every time he visited the creek he would feel shame and fear. He would worry that somebody might chase him away. The creek was off limits. From a sense of frustration he kicked a pebble out of his way. Hatred toward the woman welled up inside him. She had robbed him of the creek, the finest place he knew, and she had offended his sense of honor.

Pausing a moment, he sniffed the red roses clinging to a lamppost. He had enjoyed their fragrance on his daily walks. Today he looked around like a thief. You never knew. Somebody might not want him even smelling them. Daniel craned his neck to see the path leading to the water, then looked away. "I don't want to get chased off again," he told himself, trying hard to forget the beautiful creek.

Coming to a broken picket fence, he stopped. Daniel had passed it many times before. It belonged to the dead. The historical society had posted a sign beside it. Slowly Daniel spelled out the name: "HACIENDA CEME-TERY."

Was a cemetery public ground? He peered into the dim tangle of branches. Perhaps he could cut through them to the creek. The dead would not mind his trespassing.

The gate sagged like a tired old man. Daniel squeezed himself through it. Brown leaves crackled underfoot, and periwinkle branches, soft as angels' wings, brushed against his legs. Peace reigned among the dead—peace and quiet.

Nobody had taken care of the old cemetery for a long time. Bushes had overgrown everything, and a number of the graves had caved in. Headstones leaned. Daniel tiptoed past them until he noticed that some of the headstones had both Spanish and English inscriptions. Black letters stood out on one slim marker:

IN MEMORY OF ESLIND SELAYA.
BORN DEC. 4th, 1866.
DIED JULY 12th, 1898.
REST IN PEACE.

Daniel wondered if Eslind was a man's or a woman's name. What had the person died of? Had he or she been important? How many years had the person lived? Slowly and with great difficulty he counted on his fingers, wishing that he had spent more days at school. Teachers did teach some useful things, such as reading and counting.

"From 1866 to 1876 is ten years," Daniel figured. "Add 1876 to 1886, and you get twenty years. And 1886 to 1896 is thirty years. From 1896 to 1898 is two years. Thirty plus two equals thirty-two years." Daniel sighed with relief. He had figured it out. The person in the grave had lived thirty-two years—his mother's age.

"Imagine, dying so young!" he gasped.

Then a horrible thought struck him. What if mamma died at thirty-two? What would the family do without her? A lump caught in his throat. Mamma was sick, and sick people sometimes died. Cold chills crept over his back, and he wanted to run. He wanted to tell her he loved and needed her.

Dry sticks crackled under his feet, and tears blinded him. If only he could sit by the creek! It had always

SHOES FOR DANIEL

helped him to forget his problems, his unhappiness. But now he knew it was off limits. If only he could feel better! As a car door slammed on Bertram Road, a man's booming voice lashed into his misery. "Hey, boy, get out of there! Don't you know there are rattlesnakes in this cemetery?"

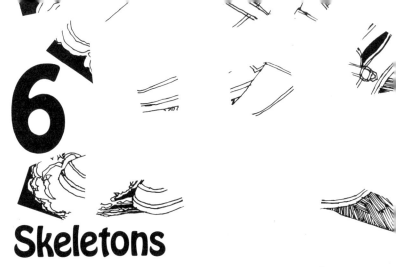

6

Skeletons

The car door slammed again, and the man drove away. Daniel was glad that he did not have to meet the man. As far as he was concerned, he would sooner take his chances with rattlesnakes than with people. The snakes only bit. People could hurt in many ways. Trudging home, he wished his family lived out of town so that he would not have to pass people.

"Why so sad, Daniel?" Linda asked him when he got home.

"Because of people," he replied sadly. "They do not want us around." He told Linda of his clash with the sharp-voiced woman.

"Poor Daniel." She tried to comfort her brother.

Linda was a good girl, he mused. Someday she would be as good as his mother. When Linda soothed him, he always felt a little better. But when mamma comforted him, she was like balm on a burn. Mamma could smooth over the fiercest pain. But now she was sick.

"Let's not tell mamma," he suggested. "She has her own troubles."

"Sí, Daniel." His sister nodded in agreement. Suddenly her face sparkled. "I want to show you some-

52

thing. Come!" She dragged him to a backyard bush.

The flicker of tiny wings made the bush seem alive. Tiny birds whirred through its branches. Some of them hung upside down in their busy search for insects. "Swee, swee, swee!" they went. The tiny creatures flitted and fluttered on the quivering branches. The whole bush stirred from their activities.

"What is the name of these birds?" Daniel whispered.

Linda shrugged. "Who knows?"

Daniel had seen carvings of similar birds decorating a relative's Christmas tree. They had round, pudgy bodies the size of a cherry tomato and long, straight tails the size of his little finger. The feathers were a dull, grayish brown. What could they be? Wild creatures were Daniel's special friends. One should know the name of his friends.

Careful not to startle them, Daniel crept closer and tried to count the flock of little birds. He nudged his sister. "These birds know how to fend for themselves, no?"

"What do you mean?" She looked blank.

"I saw a big goose the other day," he said. "It stuck its head through the fence and nibbled my fingers, wanting food."

"So?"

"The big goose could not fend for itself," Daniel patiently explained. "It cannot live without someone feeding it. Since the goose does not work, it must wait until people give it food."

"Maybe the goose is lucky people feed it, no?"

"No, Linda," he spoke softly. "When a creature does not work, it has no freedom. It has no pride. These tiny birds fly wherever they want to and feed themselves. The big goose is stuck in the yard, waiting for handouts. Which do you admire now, the birds or the goose?"

"The birds—I guess."

"Sí, Linda. I like wild creatures best because they can take care of themselves."

"Now I understand something!" A smile erupted on her puzzled face. "Size is not important. It's stamina that counts. Mrs. Henderson says that all the time."

"Mrs. Henderson is a smart woman." Daniel was glad that Linda had learned something. Sometimes he wished she could go to school.

With the creek now off limits, Daniel explored new areas. The mercury mine sprawled at the town's upper end. Daniel felt he knew the mine because of the historical markers scattered all over New Almaden.

A road led uphill beside the mine's gate. One could go as far as the NO TRESPASSING sign at the cattle guard. Daniel walked up the road until he came to the cattle guard, where he stopped to rest on a tree-shaded boulder. Green flies buzzed about his head. He beat at the pesky insects, but it did no good. More flies swarmed from the cliff wall near his seat. Wondering what was attracting them there, he stepped to the cliff's edge, only to dart back in shock.

Bleached crayfish skeletons lay scattered at the foot of the cliff, their dead eyes staring at him. Legs, antennae, and pincer claws lay tossed about. Only the tails were missing. The crayfish had died to make somebody's meal. A sob nestled in Daniel's throat as he fled the scene.

Arriving at the highway bridge, he skidded down to the water. He must know whether there were any crayfish left. Sliding to the ledge beside the water, he brushed back the willow and cottonwood branches. Strings of air bubbles welled up in the murky, deep-looking water. A rope tied to a willow trunk dropped down into the water alongside the bursting bubbles.

When he pulled up the rope, a wire basket rose to just below the surface of the water. Crayfish clung to its sides and one by one dropped off. Little fish, however, continued to nibble on pieces of bread inside the cage. They were trapped. Angrily, Daniel yanked the rope from the willow and slammed the basket against the creek bank. It sprang open. Daniel told himself, "Bueno. The crayfish will not get trapped, and the fish can swim out."

Daniel recalled his fascination at first seeing the crayfish. He had not guessed the clumsy creatures had the worst possible enemies of all—people.

"People will do anything," Daniel grumbled to himself. "They do not care if living things get killed. Nor do they care if they wipe out everything living in this creek. They only care for themselves." Daniel scrambled up to the wide spot beside the creek and sat down to stare at the water. After a while his gaze shifted to a nearby historical marker:

"Since early times a Vichy mineral spring bubbled up here beside the Alamitos Creek," he read when he approached it. "When the distant Buena Vista shaft cut vein on the 2,100-foot level, the spring ceased flowing. Wealthy San Franciscan F. L. A. Pioche commercially bottled the water in 1868 as a cure-all for the rich and thirsty. When bottled, the water lost its carbonization, and the venture also went flat financially. Across the creek stands the original mine office, built in 1850."

Daniel would have liked to drink from the spring.

Too bad the bubbly water below the bridge was dirty. He mused whether Indians had once quenched their thirst by the spring.

Deciding to investigate a sagging structure across the highway, he wondered if it was the old mine office mentioned in the historical marker. Daniel hoped the barnlike building would not collapse on top of him as he ventured into it. Wind whistled between its shrunken boards, and branches knocked against the sagging roof. He tiptoed through the weathered shingles, rusty hardware, and frayed pieces of hemp rope littering the floor.

A timeless feeling embraced him, and again he managed to forget the outside world. The wind and the scraping branches sounded like voices from a distant past. What kind of people had built the barn? He picked a nail from the dirt floor and wiped it clean. Square and irregular, the nail had been made by hand. People who came during or after the California Gold Rush had constructed the barn. They were the first to build with nails and wood in California. The Spanish and Mexicans before them had used sun-dried adobe bricks and burned tiles. And they had tied timbers with rawhide, Daniel recalled from history lessons at school.

Patches of sunlight filtered into the barn, making the floor a patchwork quilt. Lizards studied the boy a moment, then scurried away over the sun-warmed boards.

Except for the sound of creaking wood and the scuttling of field mice, the barn held great peace. Daniel peeked into a gloomy lean-to on one side of the barn. He imagined a desk in there and an important sea captain sitting behind it. The captain had come from Boston on a sailing ship around Cape Horn. At

Monterey the Spanish had given him a swift horse. Then the captain galloped to New Almaden to sit in the lean-to office and give orders.

The roar of a diesel engine jolted Daniel out of his daydream. The engine growled across the creek, and he craned his neck to see. Willows nodded beyond the barn's crossbeams, blocking his view. Daniel dashed outside into the warm sunshine behind the barn. There he looked up at two square red-brick chimneys standing on a wooded hill. A hawk drew tight circles around the old smokestacks.

The trembling willows still hid the mine. Unable to see what kind of machine was making the noise, he scaled the gravel bank to the highway. The loose gravel was hard to climb, but at last he stood on the pavement.

A sweeping view of the mine rewarded Daniel for his troubles. It sat in the canyon like an oval dishpan. Tailings or refuse lay in neat piles along the rim of the mine. Trucks and other machines stood parked beside several round metal structures and square wooden shacks. A tall crane rose and dipped into the air. He yearned to get closer to the crane to watch it work, but he honored the NO TRESPASSING signs.

Not knowing anything else to do to pass the time, he returned to Bertram Road. His feet itched to enter the path to the still spot where the crayfish lived, but his cheeks burned when he remembered the sharp-voiced woman.

On the bridge he gazed down at the creek, wishing he could dangle his feet in the cool water. Air brakes swished at the corner of Main and Bertram, and several children jumped off the school bus. A boy and a girl headed for the bridge. Suddenly feeling trapped, he wanted to slip away, but the youngsters had seen him.

Only pride kept him on the bridge.

"Hey, you! How come you don't go to school?" the boy called out.

"Who, me? I—uh, do not live here," Daniel stammered.

"What do you mean, you don't live here? We've seen you around before."

"I—uh, we're migratory workers." He wished the boy would leave him alone.

"What does your dad do?" the girl asked.

"He, uh, is a bracero."

"What's that?" she exclaimed.

"That's Mexican people who stoop over the dirt," the boy answered for Daniel.

The girl seemed surprised. "Why would anybody want to stoop over dirt?"

The boy stuck up his nose. "If you had no education, you might stoop, too," he told her.

"Doesn't your dad have an education?" she asked Daniel.

Daniel wished he had stayed at the old barn. "I—uh, do not know what you mean."

"I mean a high school diploma or college degree."

"How do you get such a thing?"

The girl giggled. "You go to school and graduate."

"My father has a high school diploma," the boy bragged. "My father has a steady job."

"My dad graduated from college," the girl said. "Daddy is a bank manager. Is your dad a college graduate?"

Daniel mopped his forehead. "I—uh, must ask him."

"What about you?" she persisted. "If you don't attend school, you won't get your high school diploma. You'll become a *dropout.*"

Squirming, Daniel felt like one already. His father said school was a waste of good working time. Children should earn money instead of sitting around. And besides, Daniel had felt out of place in the classrooms. He had attended mainly because it felt good to sit and rest instead of picking fruit or vegetables or laboring in some field. Sometimes the teacher wrote mysterious words on the blackboard. Other times he asked questions Daniel did not understand. Even so, the boy had advanced to the fourth grade. He could read and write better than his father. In a burst of confidence, he told the girl, "Maybe someday I will go to school and get my high school diploma, no?"

"Why not?" The boy and girl dashed off, laughing.

Daniel set his jaw. They were right to laugh at him, the bracero's son. *Their* fathers drove to work in suit and tie. He had seen them going by in the mornings. Papa bowed to such people. And no wonder. They were rich and had an education. Even their children spoke good English. And they all wore *shoes*. The Morales family did not belong with people like that.

Apricot Harvest

New Almaden's children puzzled Daniel. They did things he and Linda never had done. For example, they rode horses and bicycles and spoke of homework and good grades. They gave things different names. For "creek," they said "brook." A "bucket" they called a "pail." For "papa," they said "dad" or "father." Daniel did not understand them.

"I know nothing about them, and they scare me," he once told himself. "They have nice clothes and shoes, and they make me feel bad and worthless. Better to be alone than to feel bad."

The boy on the bridge had hurt Daniel's pride. If only he could show the boy that he, Daniel, could do some things better than he could! If only he could take him to the prune harvest!

Each morning Daniel had gotten up early with the family and worked from dawn to dusk. On foggy mornings they worked with the pickup lights shining on them. Daniel usually filled twenty crates by noon and another twenty by nightfall—forty crates a day.

He and his sister would have liked to have time to play. Often they said to each other, "Tonight, after work, we will make an adventure." But by quitting time they were too tired. It always had been work, work, work, until their muscles ached. Did the town's children know such feelings? Daniel wondered how many crates the boy could fill in a day. As he thought about it, a sense of pride stole into his heart which helped ease the pain of being poor.

Back on Main Street Daniel aimlessly ran his fingers over the stiff branch tips of a freshly clipped hedge. When a dog rushed to the hedge, Daniel leaped aside. It laid huge white paws on the hedge as its black eyes gazed at Daniel. The boy poised to run. Suddenly the dog seemed to grin from its pricked ear tips to its wagging tail. Standing on tiptoe, Daniel reached up and stroked the dog's coarse pelt.

"You are a beautiful white wolf, no?" he whispered into the animal's twitching ear. The dog danced on his hind feet as if happy to get attention. How could such unfriendly people own such friendly pets? The boy shook his head. It didn't make sense.

Daniel tensed when he came to the two adobe buildings. He shot sidelong glances down the drive. On the left side of the drive, a dozen yards from the sidewalk, he spotted a partially hidden sign: PRIVATE PROPERTY. DO NOT PASS OR CROSS CREEK.

A bush kept the sign almost completely out of sight from a certain angle. If only he had spotted the warning before the woman bawled him out for trespassing!

Remembering the incident, Daniel hastened through town. He didn't want to run into any more people. At the highway bridge, however, he stopped and followed a trail rambling through the weeds and disappearing under the bridge.

Under the bridge the menacing sounds of the town faded away. Only the creek babbled, and once in a while a car rolled over the bridge. Willows, tules, and cottonwoods surrounded him. Strange things could happen in such a dark and lonely place. Danger might lurk in the tangle of reeds and branches. Someone might jump out and attack him. Suddenly afraid, he splashed down the creek beneath the bridge, scrambled up the bank, and emerged on the other side of the highway.

Out in the open again, Daniel laughed. The sun shone warm and bright. Feeling safe again, he sauntered over the bridge by the Café del Río. Near St. Anthony's Church he savored the cough-drop smell of eucalyptus leaves. Looking up at the mighty trunks, he thought of himself as an ant standing beside an elephant.

Wild oats nodded on the hillside behind the church, a trail winding uphill among them. Halfway up the trail, Daniel paused to rest on a field marker. St. Anthony's Church lay below him, its steep shingle roof and tall, pointed windows nestled in the shade of the mammoth eucalypti. Cars swished over the highway bridge. Dogs barked in town. And somebody hammered in the distance.

Daniel lay on his back and stared up at the sky. A live oak spread its lacy umbrella over the trail. He blinked against the specks of sunlight filtering through the branches. Yellow finches, red-breasted linnets, and glittering hummingbirds whirred through the oak. The breeze played the oak like a giant harp.

Three great arms grew out of the tree's massive trunk. They divided and subdivided into down-curling fingerlike branches. The oak reminded Daniel of a grandfather tree. Its leaves—tough and hairy, with spiny teeth at the edges—stayed green the year round. How many summers had the oak stood? It reminded him of another question: How many summers had the earth stood, and the moon?

People had landed on the moon. Yet the moon was far, far away. Daniel chewed a grass-blade. His head felt thick with thought. "At one time America was far away," he mused. "And California was even more far."

But people had landed in America—Spanish people. He wondered how much Spanish blood flowed in his veins. Very little, he guessed. His father said the Morales family had much Mexican blood. By Mexican he probably meant Indian. But what was wrong with that? Indian was American—the original Americans. They had built great cities before the Spanish arrived and had developed one of the world's best calendars. His teachers had mentioned the Aztecs and Mayas.

"I would like to know more about those Indians," Daniel thought aloud. "And about the Spanish, too." After all, he spoke the Spanish language. He spit out the grass-blade.

"And what is wrong with speaking Spanish?" Daniel challenged the oak. Looking at the grandfatherly tree, he relaxed. "Gracias, abuelito. You make me feel better."

He skipped downhill to Main Street. The white-haired man he had helped across the street once, stood in front of his house. Seeing Daniel, he waved, "Hey, boy, check if there's something in my mailbox, will you?"

"Sí, señor." Daniel drew a letter from the box. He let a car pass by, then carried the letter to the man.

"Thank you, young feller. You saved me a trip. How about coming in? I have a nice apple for you."

"I—uh, must go home," Daniel stuttered.

"You have a minute, don't you? I'm Mr. Randall. No need to call me señor." The old man nudged the boy into his dark living room. Specks of dust whirled in the thin rays of sunshine slanting through the venetian blinds.

The elderly man pointed to a couch. "Sit down. What's your name, young feller?"

"Daniel Morales."

"Let's visit. O.K.?"

"Visit, señor?"

"It's Mr. Randall. We're in the ·United States, aren't we?" he said crisply.

"Sí, Mr. Randall." Daniel fidgeted on the couch.

"How long have you lived in Almaden, Daniel?"

"Over a month, señor—uh, Mr. Randall. We are not going to stay. We are braceros."

"Then you don't know much about New Almaden, do you?"

"No, Mr. Randall."

"Do you know how our town got founded, Daniel?"

"No."

"Do you know who started it?"

"No."

"A Mexican, Daniel."

The boy snapped to attention. "Really? Was he an important man?"

"Sure was," his new friend chuckled. "Captain Andres Castillero was a troubleshooter for the Mexican government."

"Did he ride a horse?" Daniel leaned forward.

"Sure did. Rode to Mission Santa Clara, back in 1845. At the mission, the smart captain spotted a chunk of cinnabar from our canyon. Cinnabar, you know, is the ore we get mercury from."

The boy perched on the davenport's edge. "How did the cinnabar get there?"

"Wandering Indians had carried it to the mission. You see, the Indians painted themselves with the red rock."

"What did Captain Castillero do when he saw the cinnabar?"

"He rode out to Alamitos Creek," Mr. Randall said. "When the captain saw all that red cinnabar, he called the place New Almaden, after the famous mercury mine in Spain."

"Then people came here to dig?"

"Sure did, Daniel. Mexican people and Americans, too." Mr. Randall's already pink face blushed. "We are proud of our town, Daniel. You see, without our mercury they couldn't have extracted the gold from the ore in the great gold rush. You might say it was because of Almaden's mercury that California became part of the United States. If it had not been for our town, we might not have schools where children can get a good education." He glowed with pride and excitement.

Daniel was confused, but just to say something, he mentioned the historical marker at the bridge near the Café del Río. "A sign says that two Spanish men dug for ore in the Alamitos Creek, back in 1824, Mr. Randall."

"They did." The old man nodded. "Chabolla and Sunol dug for silver and found none. Shows you how you can pass up riches if you look for the wrong thing. It's like living near a school and not attending it." Mr. Randall gave him an apple. "Come back again, Daniel. Check my mailbox when you do."

"Sí, Mr. Randall. Gracias." Daniel's head whirred like a beehive. The old man told fine stories, liked company, and trusted him, Daniel, with the mail. How could this be? On his way home the boy tried to figure it out.

When he got home, he found his mother sitting on the bed, feet propped high. "Here, Mamma, this beautiful apple, it is for you."

"Muchas gracias, Daniel." She tousled his hair and smiled at her husband, who sat on a fruit crate.

"Where did you get the apple, Daniel?" papa inquired.

"From Mr. Randall." He explained the circumstances.

Señor Morales was again out of a job. One morning the pickup had not started, causing papa to miss a day's work. His boss had then fired him. Mamma's legs remained swollen, and her health had worsened with the onset of hot weather. She slept much lately. Sometimes she lay in bed without paying attention even to Angelina.

Except for mealtimes and taking care of the vegetable patch, Daniel hated to stay home. His mother's plight upset him greatly. He wished he could help her, but he feared that if he stayed around the house, she might sense his sadness.

As the rent came due, the landlord threatened to throw the family out. Fortunately, papa found a job as janitor. It did not pay much, but it provided steady employment. He managed to pay another month's rent just in time.

Daniel obtained an apricot harvesting job out in the valley. On his way to work papa dropped him off at the grower's open shed, where the boy worked with several cutters. The cutters halved the ripe apricots, removed the pits, and placed the fruit face up on wooden trays.

Daniel emptied the fruit crates and filled the trays.

The grower stacked the full trays on a cart. Before loading it, he inspected the trays. Daniel's apricots lay evenly spaced, their sides touching like the parts of a honeycomb. "You do good work, Daniel," the man complimented.

"Gracias, señor." Daniel helped lift the full trays onto the cart. Although they weighed only some ten to twenty pounds, they were awkward to carry. Yet he worked fast enough that before the orchard owner could stop at the next cutter's, the boy had lugged another empty tray onto his sawhorses.

The grower stacked the fruit-covered trays ten inches high and rolled the bulky cart into the sulfur shed. Daniel knew that sulfur preserved the fruit's golden color. After four to eight hours, the owner of the orchard removed the trays from the shed and spread them out in the sun. Every morning Daniel looked with pride at the field covered with golden fruit.

Four days later the grower "stagger-stacked" the trays. The wind dried the apricots another four to six days. And all the while the pickers leaned their ladders against the trees, filled their buckets with apricots, and shook the ripe fruit into the waiting crates.

For every filled tray, the grower's wife punched the cutter's card. Soon Daniel's card bristled with holes, but his fingers felt raw from the fruit juices.

The owner of the orchard paid a bonus for the pits. His wife explained to Daniel that he sold them to a large processing company in San Jose, which extracted oils from the kernels for the food, perfume, and cosmetic industries. The ground-up shells made sandblasting compounds and other abrasives.

At the end of the cutting season the grower's wife

paid everybody off. Daniel rejoiced that he had earned money all by himself. In the shade of a harvested tree he waited for his father. As soon as the pickup stopped, he bounded into the cab. Shoving a twenty-dollar bill and change into his father's hand, he exclaimed, "Here, Papa; this will pay for beans and gasoline."

"You are a good son, Daniel. God bless you." Pride made golden flecks in the father's warm brown eyes.

Time had moved fast when he worked in the cutting shed. But now, with his job over, suddenly it seemed to stand still. He decided to stop by and visit Mr. Randall again. The day after the apricot season ended, the mail arrived late. Daniel pulled a bunch of junk mail from Mr. Randall's box and carried it to the house. Grinning, the old man opened the door wide. "Haven't seen you in ages, Daniel. Were you on vacation?"

"Vacation?" The boy's mind was blank.

"School is out, isn't it?"

"I—uh, guess so. I never did go to school here."

"Why not?" A frown settled on his rosy face. After listening to Daniel's explanation, he took several framed photos from a shelf. "These are my sons and grandsons, Daniel. They were fine boys like you, but they went to school."

"Did they become somebody important?" He contemplated the well-dressed men in the photos.

"Sure did, Daniel! Every one of them. You could become important, too, if you'd attend school. Education is a key to future success."

"What could I be?" Daniel asked eagerly.

"A doctor, lawyer, executive, anything. You can be *anybody* with the proper preparation."

Mr. Randall's words echoed in Daniel's ears even

as he ran to the post office to buy stamps for the old man. The post office was located in La Casa Grande, Almaden's proud old two-story red-brick mansion. Its white columns cast black shadows on the front porch, while high above the roof, lanky fan palms waved in the breeze.

For weeks the building had dozed quietly, a trickle of people walking up the steps to the post office, the shops, or the art museum. Today music and happy shouts came from the yard surrounding it. Daniel ran to the tall wire fence beside the mansion to see what was going on.

Two great blue basins sparkled between the nodding trees. The town's swimming pools had opened, and Almaden's children splashed in the water.

Daniel walked away from the fence, knowing that he would never get to swim there. He owned no swimsuit, and he had no money to pay the woman at the gate.

Attacked

Daniel turned his back toward the swimming pools, the youngsters' happy shouts drumming in his ears and mocking him for being poor, and plodded into the post office. He laid Mr. Randall's money on the counter. "A book of stamps, please."

"Here you are." The postmaster exchanged the money for stamps, which Daniel tucked into the pocket of his faded shirt. Then he stepped out into the dazzling sun, thinking, "The postmaster is an important man. Without stamps, Mr. Randall couldn't write letters to his grandsons. What would it take to become a postmaster?"

Voices rose and fell under the shops' red and white awnings. A woman left the beauty shop, her high-heeled shoes clicking on the steps as she headed for a parked yellow sports car. The motor growled, and its wheels crunched on the gravel as she drove up to Main Street. Daniel waited until the dust it stirred up had settled. What did her husband do for a living? he wondered. "He has education, for he makes much money," Daniel decided. His mother never visited beauty shops. She could spare no money for frills, and she certainly owned no car to drive to them. Daniel trudged to the

70

street and paused by another of the town's historical markers:

"Casa Grande. Built in 1854 of adobe, brick, and wood. Residence of Mine Manager until 1925. Most stately and gracious California mansion of early days. Scene of important social and political events. Planned by Henry W. Halleck and built by J. Young & F. Meyer. Halleck was General-in-Chief, Union Armies in Civil War."

So the mansion had seen important people, he mused. Surely a general had much, much education, he reasoned as he took the stamps to Mr. Randall. He wanted to ask the old man some questions about Casa Grande, but did not dare. Mr. Randall might get annoyed as other people did when he inquired about something.

Not knowing how to pass any more time, Daniel headed for the grandfather oak on the hillside. From the road, the oak blended in with the other trees. You did not realize what a fine tree it was until you stood underneath it.

"If you want to become somebody other than a field worker, you have to get an education, such as going to school and getting a high school diploma," Daniel sighed to himself. He contemplated the oak's massive trunk, its maze of boughs and branches. It would take five men with arms outstretched to reach completely around it. It would take the brains of five braceros to become somebody important, he angrily thought to himself. Stooping over furrows was simpler than learning. He, Daniel, would never amount to anything more than a fruit picker.

Perhaps even the oak was smarter than he. It was a big tree when Indian men hunted game and Indian women gathered seeds into baskets beneath it. The oak had seen the two Spanish men who dug for ore in Alamitos Creek. If it could speak, the tree would tell finer stories than human grandfathers could ever do. It knew tales of Indians, Spaniards—and Mexicans, too.

Some rustling sounds uphill nudged Daniel out of his daydream. A doe lifted her head, her black ear tips standing out against the leaves. Her liquid eyes studied the boy. Then, without haste, she disappeared, every step spelling dignity.

Perhaps next time, Daniel hoped, the doe would stay. Animals sensed whether you meant harm or not. He followed the doe, listening for sounds that might indicate its location. The tracks led above the oak to a concrete irrigation canal. The canal was empty since the winter rains had washed the concrete surface clean. But on the other side he found the doe's heart-shaped tracks again and followed them over a culvert and around a sun-baked hill.

Other tracks also showed in the dust: large paw marks, small handlike prints, tiny spurred impressions. Excitedly he realized that wild animals used the path. During the night they came down to drink from the creek.

The path grew steep, and the sun broiled down. Daniel turned back, walking in his own footsteps so as not to disturb the animal tracks. Lizards scurried through dry leaves, and a rabbit nibbled in the brush. Some large animal broke through the bushes above the canal. Daniel liked the place. Feeling as happy as a kitten, he curled his toes in the soft red earth.

A diesel motor barked at the mine below. Daniel shaded his eyes against the sun to see where it was. The crane arm of a dredge reared up, its bucket dangling from it like a giant clam. The bucket's jaws bit into a stand of willows growing between an algae-covered pond and the creek. A willow trunk crunched between the bucket's teeth. The operator let the bucket plummet down and dig deep into the hillside. Daniel squatted to watch the bucket lift the uprooted willows and dump them beside the pond.

What was the purpose of uprooting trees? He did not understand what was happening. The dredge's cables strained, and the bucket grabbed more willows. The dangling trees and branches scraped the cliff as the dredge lifted them to one side. Finally dirt and dust hovered in a cloud as the bucket emptied its load.

The dredge rolled over the bank on caterpillar tracks, seeming to topple for a moment. Daniel admired the operator's skill, but he realized that something had gone wrong with the machine when the man jumped from his seat to check the bucket. The boy wished he could control such a great machine. What did it take to become master of such a big thing?

The sound of hoofbeats sent Daniel hurtling behind a bush. Two teen-agers rode around the bend on horses. He hid until they passed. He did not want to get chased off again as he had been at the creek.

When the riders had disappeared, he glanced back in the direction of the mine. The bucket on the dredge seemed stuck. He decided to retrace his steps. Around the bend he inhaled the breeze coming up from San Francisco Bay. One could always count on it. The Bay was the valley's natural air conditioning.

Near the Hacienda Cemetery Daniel slowed his steps. A gray-haired woman stepped out of a nearby house. Behind her hopped a blonde ten-year-old girl, her pink-ribboned braids flopping against her shoulders.

Both headed for a car parked beside the cemetery's white picket fence. Apparently having forgotten something, the woman turned back to the house. Daniel walked on.

Minutes later she drove up the road. Daniel stepped aside, letting the car pass. The girl pressed her face against the car window, looking at Daniel. For a split second Daniel thought the girl smiled. But who would smile at a ragged boy like him?

The creek gurgled and splashed below the road. Daniel missed going to the quiet spot where the crayfish lay. He caught a glimpse of the creek from the road. Sun spots danced on the water, while fish darted beneath the surface, casting shadows which looked like more fish. Watching the submerged rocks, he saw nothing moving in the water that might be crayfish. Reluctantly he fought the temptation to slide down the bank to the creek. He didn't want the woman or someone else to chase him away.

Sun and shade splashed mosaiclike patterns on the pavement—patterns that changed with the different times of day. But always they were beautiful.

Beautiful, too, were the berry bushes at the few open spots along the creek. Blackberries crowded each other on the arching vines. For months, red berries and purplish-white blossoms had smothered the bushes. Ripe berries now sparkled on them like Angelina's laughing eyes.

Angelina loved berries. Daniel popped one into his mouth. It tasted sweet. He decided to take some home to his sister, but didn't know what to put them in. Scanning the road, he saw a garbage can standing a short distance from a house. A rock weighted down its lid. As he heaved the rock aside, several dogs at the house yapped at once. Frightened, Daniel darted behind a lone redwood.

A squirrel sitting on a branch above him scolded the boy's presence. Its forepaws tapped the bark of the branch, and its tail jerked. Daniel chuckled. The roar of passing cars chased the squirrel up the tree. And with Daniel gone, the dogs quit yapping.

The boy headed for the Café del Río. In one of the restaurant's garbage cans he found a plastic sandwich bag. With the bag swinging from his hand, he returned to the berry patch, thinking how Angelina would clap her hands at seeing the berries.

He gathered what ripe berries he could reach from the road, then slid down the bank. Breaking through the thorny vines, Daniel flushed out three large, brownish-blue birds—mourning doves. The explosive whir of their wings startled him.

Car doors slammed at the house above the road, and a young woman walked toward the front door carrying a grocery sack. Daniel ducked, too late. She had seen him. Stepping to the edge of the road, she called, "Are you picking berries?"

"Sí, señora." He felt sick inside at the prospect of another scolding from an Anglo woman.

"What do you do with them?"

"I give them to my baby sister. She's crazy about berries."

"You mean you're not eating them yourself?"

"No, señora." He held up the half-filled bag.

The woman's face softened. "Go ahead and fill the bag. You can pick all you want."

"Gracias, señora." Daniel felt like crying. He was not used to people who were not de la raza being nice. Tonight he would remember her in his prayers.

Birds twittered in the trees like girls sharing secrets with each other. Daniel too had a secret to tell. Some Anglo people were nice to bracero boys. He felt warm, content, peaceful. The sun shimmered on the creek, the golden reflections flickering on the berry bushes. Leaves rustled in the breeze. At last, legs and arms scratched, the plastic bag filled, he started homeward.

Passing a house with a carport, he suddenly tensed. A large German shepherd dog lifted his head and watched him. At first the dog had lain at the end of his chain without showing much interest. Then his eyes had followed Daniel. A warning sign bristled at the gate: BEWARE OF DOG!

You never knew about dogs. Some were harder to figure out than others. This one, however, didn't bark or rattle its chain. Daniel passed at the far side of the road. Somehow the watchdog didn't look fierce. Something else showed in its face—sadness.

"He is lonely," Daniel thought to himself. "The chestnut colt, the little goat, the fluffy cat—they were lonely, too."

On Main Street the pepper trees rippled in the breeze. Daniel broke off a feathery leaf, crushed it between thumb and forefinger, and sniffed. The spicy fragrance reminded him of leather. And leather made him think of shoes. Sighing, he tossed the leaf away.

Angelina met him at the door. "Look what I have for you!" he said, dangling the plastic sack over her button nose.

"Berries!" she crowed.

"Eat them!" He opened the bag for her.

Daniel brought home whatever food he could find for his sister and mother. He took them apricots while they lasted, plus what he picked up from the restaurant's garbage cans. His own stomach had shrunk since the family began living at New Almaden. By the time his father paid for rent, gasoline, and water and electricity, they had little money left for food.

Angelina waddled to her mother and sat on the bed to eat the berries. Linda watched the toddler from the kitchen. "Look at the baby!" she chuckled. "She's purple from the berries." Whenever Mrs. Henderson gave Linda a cookie or something else to eat, she also saved it for her little sister. In the afternoons, she dragged Angelina around the house and yard as she would a doll.

Linda was a big help to her mother. Señora Morales could not get along without her. In addition, Daniel swept the cabin and sometimes washed the window so that mamma could watch the squirrels.

She could not stand the sun anymore, and the hot weather confined her to the house. He missed his mother's laughter and songs. Her illness hung over the family like a black cloud of an approaching storm. Daniel felt crushed in her presence. Outdoors, however, he always felt a little better.

Each day the boy checked the dredge's progress at the mine. One day, to his disappointment, he noticed the crane standing idle. The pond had vanished, the algae-covered water having emptied into the creek. A bulldozer snorted and rattled around, shoving dirt into piles. The operator bounced on his seat, a cap and visor shielding his head from dust and sun. Daniel admired the operator. "He is a smart hombre, that one," he whispered to himself. "He has learned how to operate big machines."

The heat of the sun drove the boy from the hill. Walking in the shade of the oaks, laurel, and sycamores, Daniel followed the highway. Today he would explore!

He passed two riding stables and a cluster of houses. Dogs barked menacingly in one of the garages. After crossing a high bridge spanning Alamitos Creek, he puffed uphill.

When he reached the crest, he could see a dam holding back a man-made lake which filled the upper canyon. Two youths stood fishing along the edge of the water. Daniel watched awhile, but the boys did not look his way.

The highway snaked along the edge of the reservoir and up the canyon. He pressed on, wanting to learn where the highway went. The sun glared down on him. Tall cliffs shut out the cooling breezes from San Francisco Bay. The pavement scorched the soles of his bare feet. Finally he decided to turn back.

Sun spots glimmered on the lake like a million stars, shooting into his eyes like burning darts. The boy shielded his eyes against the glare, but it did not help much.

Once past the reservoir, Daniel could again embrace the cool Bay breeze. Nor did he have to squint as much. He leaned over the iron guardrail on the high bridge and watched the creek gurgle far below.

Near the cluster of houses, a car zoomed past him and sped downhill after veering to the wrong side of the road. Daniel leaped off the shoulder of the road. Since drivers often lost control on the roads winding through the hills, he decided to be more careful. Then, before he knew what had happened, three dogs shot out of a yard and attacked him. Barking, snapping, growling, they chased him back onto the hot pavement.

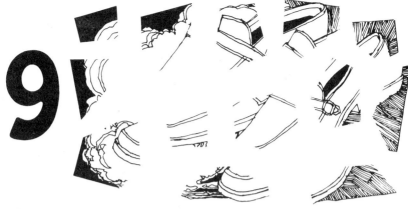

A High School Diploma?

The fierce dogs held Daniel at bay. Barking, snapping, jumping, they seemed determined to tear him apart. Desperately he tried to get off the road, for he feared the next car shooting downhill might flatten him. But the moment he started for the shoulder of the road, he felt two searing bites in his right leg. The smallest and fiercest dog had bitten through his jeans. Suddenly Daniel panicked. He could not shake the three dogs, nor could he leave the road.

After what seemed like hours, a woman emerged from the house below the road and called the dogs away.

Daniel limped to the drive. "That little brown dog bit me twice," he told the woman.

"It did?" The woman's thin eyebrows arched in surprise. "She has pups, but she won't stay with them."

Standing on the stone slab in front of the house, he fought back his tears. The woman took him by the arm and packed the boy into her car. As they raced downhill, she asked him where he lived. Daniel directed her to the cabin.

"Your father must come with us," she declared as she parked the car by the house. "Is he at home?"

79

"No, señora. Papa works in San Jose."

"What about your mother?" Without waiting for his answer, the woman stormed into the house. "Are you the boy's mother?" she asked the sick woman on the bed.

"Sí, señora. Is something wrong?" Señora Morales struggled up from the mattress.

"My dog bit him. You must come along to the hospital."

"Hospital?" mamma screeched. "We have no money."

"Never mind the money. Let the insurance worry about the bill." The woman dragged her to the car, then they sped to a San Jose hospital, where she unloaded them by the emergency room.

The receptionist asked a string of questions, which they answered. Then all three sat and waited with other people in the long hall. Finally a nurse called his name.

"Daniel Morales?"

"Here, señora." Daniel and his mother followed the nurse into a tiny room. The nurse faced the boy.

"When have you had your last tetanus shot?"

"I—uh, do not know what you mean." He looked at his mother for assistance.

"What is tetanus?" mamma asked.

"Everybody knows what tetanus is," the nurse stated. "Think hard. When did the boy have his last shot?"

"Nobody in our family has had such shots," mamma said.

"Are you sure?" The nurse scrutinized Daniel's mother.

"Sí."

"Wait here! I'll be right back." The nurse left,

to return in a few minutes with a doctor.

"Are you Mrs. Morales?" the doctor inquired, studying her.

"Sí, señor doctor." Mamma looked bewildered.

"May I?" The doctor pressed his fingers against her legs.

She pointed to Daniel. "He is the one with the dog bite."

"I know." The doctor kept on examining her legs. "How long have you had this swelling?" he asked.

"Since last spring. It is nothing important. It goes away when I sit with my legs up." She seemed terribly embarrassed.

"What other problems do you have?"

Confused, she answered, "None, señor doctor."

"She cannot breathe, and she cannot work," Daniel blurted out. "Help her, señor doctor! Mamma is sick."

"You must come to my office, Mrs. Morales. The nurse will give you my card. About your son——" The physician turned to Daniel. "The nurse tells me he never has received any tetanus injections. Is that true?"

"Sí." Mamma nodded.

"He needs some now, Mrs. Morales. It's for his protection. And he'll need booster shots later on." The doctor inspected the back of Daniel's right leg. The skin was broken, but no blood showed at the two puncture wounds. Finished with the examination, the man gave instructions to the nurse.

She filled two hypodermic needles with clear liquid and thrust one into each of Daniel's arms. It was quick and did not hurt. When the hypos were empty, she removed the needle and dabbed the pierced skin with alcohol. Then Daniel pressed the moist cotton swabs against his arms.

"When you get home, young man, be sure to wash out your dog bites," the nurse instructed him. "Swish the soap around with lots of water. O.K.?"

"Am I through?"

"Yes, you're all through," she replied with a smile.

"Gracias, señora." He led his mother to the hall. She seemed glad they were leaving the hospital. The waiting woman drove them home.

"I'll take the dog and pups for the rabies check first thing in the morning," she assured Señora Morales.

"Muchas gracias, señora." Mamma still seemed shaken from the trip as he led her into the house. At the door she stopped to let her heartbeat catch up with her breathing. "I should be the one to lead you, Daniel," she gasped. "You are the one who is hurt."

He shook his head. "No, Mamma. I feel fine."

But during the rest of the week Daniel did not feel so well. Sometimes he shivered in the sunshine. Other times he perspired in the shade. Mamma said the liquid the nurse had injected into his arms probably produced his odd sensations.

Several weeks later the owner of the dog drove Daniel to San Jose for his first booster shot. He and his father had pleaded with Mamma to also see the doctor. Yielding to the pressure, she accompanied the boy. While he waited to be called, mamma tapped at the nurse's window. "I wish to see the señor doctor," she told the young woman.

The nurse glanced up from the papers on the counter in front of her. "Do you have an appointment?"

"What is 'appointment'?"

"You must tell me when you can come in."

Surprise in her voice, Daniel's mother exclaimed, "I am in now."

"The doctor has other patients today," the nurse explained. "They made their appointments weeks ago."

"Then I make an appointment now," mamma said solemnly.

"Fill out this form, please." The nurse handed a long sheet of paper through the window.

Mamma passed it to her son to read. He stared at the difficult-to-read and harder-to-understand fine print. Handing the form to the nurse, he said, "I do not read so well, señora. Can you help?"

"Of course." She assisted them in filling out the form. Then she made an appointment for Señora Morales on the day of Daniel's second booster shot. Mamma tucked the little card into the pocket of her full skirt.

At home, when she struggled out of the car, Daniel thought his mother had gained much weight around the middle. But how could that be? he wondered. Mamma did not eat much. She saved every morsel for the children.

After Daniel's booster shot, the canyon brooded in the summer heat. But Daniel took walks anyway. Out on the buckling brick sidewalk, in the shade of the trees, he worried less about his mother.

Mr. Randall suffered from the heat almost as much as his mother. He seemed glad that Daniel saved him the walk to the mailbox. During the cooler days Mr. Randall had told stories of New Almaden's past, or he had urged Daniel to attend school. Now he sat mostly in his living room, fanning his flushed face.

Main Street was hot, but Bertram Road was even hotter. Cats sprawled on porches, and dogs stretched their legs on grassy spots. The collie, who usually answered Daniel's call with his wagging tail, lay beside the road, too hot to frolic about. The squirrels, though active, moved without haste. One squirrel paused mid-way up a tree trunk as Daniel approached. Only a few feet away from the boy, it flicked its bushy tail, then climbed slowly upward. Perching on a branch, it scratched behind an ear. A second squirrel scampered across the road. Daniel watched them both until they disappeared in the foliage.

Stopping near the picnic benches by the Café del Río, Daniel scanned the creek. Foul odors lingered over the water, and flies buzzed on the green scum. Under the highway bridge upstream a family sitting on folding stools tried to cool off. Daniel longed to visit the still spot where the water ran clear.

He entered the trail leading to the grandfather oak, spotting tracks of small, cloven hooves, each about a foot apart. Every night the deer ventured down to the water. A man's shoe prints and the impression of horses' hooves had blurred some of the tracks.

A breeze played in the oak. The scent of herbs filled the hillside air with fragrance. Unseen animals scurried through the dry grasses. Daniel relaxed on a boulder.

A motor started up behind St. Anthony's Church, its roar disrupting the peaceful quiet. He decided to investigate the noise and found a backhoe digging a hole in someone's front yard. Daniel wanted to ask the operator what the hole was for. A well? A mine for cinnabar ore? The machine's operator frowned as he concentrated on his work.

"Maybe I had better not get too close," he told himself. "The man might bawl me out." He watched from a distance as the man scooped dirt up and dumped the load on a mound beside the drive. Perspiring almost as much as the backhoe operator, Daniel headed down

Main Street, hoping to catch a breeze.

The Stars and Stripes and the California bear flag waved side by side above the firehouse. The flag reminded Daniel of Mr. Randall. The old man said Mexican-American children and Anglo children could attend school side by side for mutual benefit. Daniel pondered what the words "mutual benefit" meant. He guessed that they indicated something that was good for both.

The red fire truck stood in its barn, ready to roar off to fight some blaze. Paths crisscrossed the hillside beside the station itself. Daniel decided to explore them. Wild oats rustled under his feet as he climbed up the hill. When he reached the top, he embraced the wind that rippled along the crest. The hill made a fine lookout point. Below he could see the town snaking along the creek. The roofs of its houses peeked from under the trees. Brush and trees covered the hill beyond the town. He breathed deeply, then followed the maze of paths.

In the center of the hillside, Daniel stumbled over an oak sapling. He studied the hillside. The nearest oak stood a long way downhill. Where had the sapling come from? Had a woodpecker lost the acorn? Or a squirrel forgotten its cache?

Puzzled, Daniel waded through the oats to the fence bordering the fire station. Monterey pines extended their shade-giving arms over it. He gazed back at the dusty green sapling in the center of the hillside. The little oak stood in a better spot than many a larger tree. It would grow great branches and not have to compete for sunlight. Daniel closed his eyes and imagined himself an acorn.

A woodpecker snatched him from a squirrel. Then

the bird lost him in a meadow. Winter showers put roots on him, and he rose above the ground. Dewdrops glittered on his leaves. Green grasses hugged him. Golden poppies smiled a springtime welcome. Daniel stretched toward the sun—grew and grew. Birds flashed through his branches, and squirrels built nests in his crown. Does placed their spotted babies in grassy shelters near his trunk. The wild creatures came to him for food and shelter. He felt wanted and important, for he helped others. Then his dream vanished like a pricked bubble, and his arms dropped to his sides.

"What a fool I am!" Daniel scolded himself. "How can a fruit picker ever really help others?" Such daydreams were too good to come true. Shaking his head, he headed for the mercury mine. A car stopped on the shoulder of the road behind him. When Daniel looked back, the young driver smiled at him from behind a shaggy beard. "Want a ride?" he asked.

"No, gracias."

"Sorry." The foreign car, painted in bright abstract designs, pulled back on the road and vanished in a cloud of dust. Daniel wondered why the driver had offered him a ride. Could he not see that Daniel was only a fruit picker's son?

Puzzled, the boy turned into Main Street. NEW ALMADEN STORE, BUILT OF ADOBE IN 1849, declared large letters on the side of one old building. As he passed the store's entrance, he wondered what they sold. His father bought the family's food in San Jose—beans and flour mostly.

Trees crowded each other behind the store. Along the creek the saplings struggled to reach the sun. Daniel felt sorry for the young trees because they had no place to grow freely.

The young oak on the hillside was luckier. It would become a fine tree. With a bit of help, it had found a choicer spot than the parent tree. Daniel wondered if such a miracle could happen to a human child. What kind of help could a Chicano expect? Education maybe? He must ask his father.

"Go to school and become somebody important?" Papa's jaw dropped at his son's question. "School is not for us, Daniel. Our people have always been braceros. When mamma gets well, we must move on and go after the crops."

"But you have a job, Papa. You're a janitor."

"Rolando Morales, he does not wish to push a broom the rest of his life," papa finally answered.

"If I go to school, I could ride the bus, Papa. I could earn a high school diploma."

"A high school diploma?" Señor Morales seemed shocked. "People like us do not learn so good, Daniel."

"God made the bracero's head the same size as other people's. Perhaps he gave him a brain, too," the boy reasoned.

"No, Daniel. The teacher gets angry when you don't know nothing. The kids make fun of you. I know." Papa sighed. "You do not want this to happen, do you, Daniel?"

Hoping that his father would not think him disrespectful, Daniel replied, "If I do not learn so good, I can still try, Papa."

"You have no shoes. When children go to school, they should wear shoes." Papa sadly tousled his son's hair.

A dry, scratchy lump pushed into Daniel's throat. If only his father would understand! But papa had made his decision. His word was law.

A High School Diploma?   87

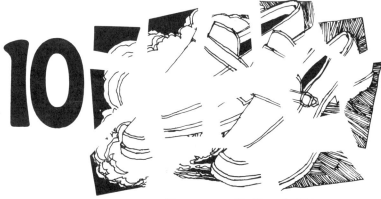

Language Is a Mailbox

On the day of Daniel's second booster shot, mamma brushed her long hair until it gleamed. She took her good dress from the fruit crate, only to put it back when it did not fit around her waist. Nor did the sandals papa had brought from San Jose slip over her swollen feet. When the woman who owned the dog that had bit Daniel stopped by with the car, mamma wore her full skirt and no shoes.

"Do not concern yourself, my son," she told him. "Shoes or no shoes, the doctor will give the checkup, and that is the main thing."

She stayed in the doctor's office a long time. When she came out, she looked very old.

"What's wrong, Mamma?" Daniel whispered on the way to the car. "What did the doctor tell you?"

"We will talk about that later. Papa must hear it, too." She eased herself into the car. On the ride home she appeared to gaze unseeingly at the scenery of the Almaden Valley.

"Poor mamma!" Daniel thought. She seemed worn out from a lifetime of hardships. He wondered if his mother had ever been a girl. Compared to the woman driving the car, she looked like a grandmother.

Once home, mamma immediately went to bed and lay there—still dressed—like a person in shock. Daniel fretted until his father came home.

"What did the doctor say?" Señor Morales kept asking until his wife at last answered.

"He said my heart is bad," she replied like somebody without any feeling.

Papa adjusted her pillows. "Did the doctor give you medicine?"

Daniel thought his father was hiding his shock well.

"He gave me this," she said, pulling a prescription out of her skirt pocket.

With anxiety in his voice, he inquired, "Will the medicine make you well?"

Mamma shook her head. "The doctor said I need an operation."

"On the heart?" He drew back.

"Sí. The doctor said I must go to the hospital for a big checkup. The surgeons need to know more about my heart before they can operate."

"Such an operation—is it dangerous?" The muscles in his face twitched.

"Sí. The doctor says one patient out of twenty may die. He says not to worry about that because——"

"Because what?"

"Because, he says that without the operation I will die anyway."

Señor Morales was silent a moment. "When did the doctor say to go in for the checkup?"

Mamma kept her voice steady. "He wants me to go now."

"What—did you tell him?"

"I said we must talk this over in the family."

"I will call the doctor." Papa's Adam's apple bobbed

up and down as he seemed to have difficulty swallowing. He securely tucked the prescription into the pocket of his open shirt.

Mamma grasped his arm. "Please do not call," she said. "The operation costs much money. The children will starve. Get the medicine. It will help for a little while."

"I will buy the medicine. We will talk about the operation later." His gentle voice seemed to relax her, and she released her grip on his arm. He roared off in the pickup to a San Jose drugstore, returning with two small bottles.

Holding them out to his wife, he said, "Take the pills now so you get better quick."

She shook her head. "The doctor said to take them in the morning."

For breakfast the next day mamma ate her food unsalted. She was on a salt-free diet. After breakfast she swallowed two tiny pills. Daniel wondered how anything so small could possibly help her. He watered the vegetable patch and waited for his mother to get well. But nothing drastic happened. She simply sat on the bed, watching Angelina. Feeling like a bubble about to burst, he asked, "Will you be all right, Mamma?"

"Sí, Daniel. Go and have fun." Mamma waved absentmindedly at him, wrapped up in her thoughts.

"Gracias, Mamma." Aching with worry, Daniel left the house. Walking awhile helped make him feel a little better.

A flock of gray birds flew low over Main Street, making strange cries. Daniel watched as the flock swept past one bird lying on the road. The boy's throat tightened. Was the bird injured? Dead? He lifted the still creature. Its eyes were shut, but the feathers were clean.

No blood showed anywhere. Had a car struck the bird, or had it died of natural causes?

The flock whirred about Daniel's head, their cries sounding like pleas for help.

"I am sorry, little birds. I cannot help your friend."

The dead bird had a yellow breast and pink underside. A black wedge, underlined by a white speck, surrounded the eye. The large bird filled his hand. He spread its toes apart. No longer would they hop in the grass or cling to a hedge. Pulling a rag from his pocket, he wrapped it like a shroud around the still creature. The gray birds chattered on nearby power lines, watching him. And they escorted him to the grandfather oak.

"This bird can no longer fly, abuelito," Daniel told the oak. "I want you to watch over it and give it shelter."

Daniel buried the bird beneath the oak. His chest felt heavy like stone. He thought of his mother and the fact that she would die without an operation.

Downhill, near St. Anthony's Church, he remembered the kind girl who had smiled at him as she rode past. He had not seen the black-haired rider again. Daniel guessed she lived out in the valley.

Honking cars rolled into the Café del Río's parking lot. Pink and white streamers fluttered around the lead car, and tin cans clattered and bounced on the pavement behind. A wedding party was about to begin.

Food smells drifted from the restaurant. The historical marker said the del Río had been built in 1848 as California's first two-story adobe hotel. Travelers considered that it served the best meals in the West. "As inviting as those served now," the sign claimed. Daniel wondered what they were preparing for the wedding dinner. It was not anything he knew. He'd check the garbage cans after dark. Big parties always wasted much food. Daniel knew he would not find chili peppers, tortillas, beans, or tamales in the cans. The del Río didn't cook anything like that. Its patrons favored different kinds of food. And no wonder—they were different kinds of people.

Daniel had watched the people of New Almaden ever since his family arrived in the town. They did things in unfamiliar ways. Curious, he wondered which way was better—that of his family or that of the towns-people. Perhaps Mr. Randall would know. He would ask him.

Mr. Randall's mailbox contained no mail, but the old man waved to him from his window. Daniel raced across the street as Mr. Randall held the door open. "What's the hurry, Daniel?"

"I—uh, came to ask you something."

"Yes, Daniel?" Mr. Randall leaned forward on his cane.

"Which food is better, Mexican or American?"

"Which food do *you* like better?"

"Mexican."

"Then that's the best food for you." The man laughed.

"Then which language is better, Spanish or English?" Suddenly Daniel wished he hadn't asked.

Mr. Randall's blue eyes no longer twinkled. "Either language is fine, Daniel. Two languages are better."

The boy squirmed. "You mean—it is all right to speak Spanish?"

"Of course it is all right."

Daniel felt confused. "But—you said not to call you señor. And kids have teased me for speaking Spanish."

With jerky steps Mr. Randall crossed to his bookcase. He took a framed photo from a shelf and showed it to Daniel. "This is my mother, Daniel. She came from a foreign country. Mother could not speak English when she came to the United States. But she learned our language so that everybody could understand her. Once she knew the English word for something, she used it all the time. One day she visited the old country. Then she spoke only German." He returned the picture to the shelf.

"You see, Daniel, a language is like a mailbox. It helps the communication between people. When you speak Spanish around here, nobody understands you. And, on the other hand, some of your family might not know what you were saying if you used only English. You want people to know what you say, don't you?"

"I—uh, never thought of it that way before," Daniel stuttered. "But what about the other things people do different from my family?"

"There are good things about your people, and about mine," the elderly man replied. "We could learn from each other and profit from it."

"Can you profit by me?"

Mr. Randall chuckled at the boy's eagerness. "Sure, Daniel. You save me the trip across the street. And you keep me company. Lonely old people don't find considerate fellers like you very often, you know."

"My pleasure." With a glow of pride Daniel realized that somebody outside of his own family actually wanted him. And Mr. Randall shared his wisdom with him, the bracero boy. He was the finest person Daniel had known outside his own family. Daniel wanted to tell him about his mother, but, afraid to overstay his welcome, he left.

Before he reached home, he met Linda, bouncing down the street. Only ten years old, she did not understand the family's troubles. Daniel was glad for that. Together they walked to their cabin. "Are you feeling better, Mamma?" they asked in unison.

She smiled at them. "Sí, the pills are working."

"How can you tell?" Linda asked.

"The swelling is going down." She showed them her ankles, which did look less puffy.

Linda joyfully clasped her brother's hands and squealed, "Mamma is better!" Brother and sister whirled through the cabin in their joy. They could not wait to tell their father the good news.

Papa came home late, bringing used mattresses for Linda and Daniel. He dumped them in opposite corners of the porch.

Linda hopped up and down on hers. "Look, Daniel, I can jump!" she announced.

Daniel tried his own mattress. The springs sagged. Suddenly he remembered mamma. "We must not make noise, Linda. Mamma is sick."

"Oh, I forgot." She went for her pillow and blanket, while her brother readied his own bed for the night.

At nightfall he headed for the garbage cans behind the Café del Río. Its neon sign glowed red. Music and laughter filled the building. Daniel stole into the dimly lighted side yard. Lifting the lids off the cans, he inspected their contents. Whatever seemed edible, he tossed into a sack. Then, tucking the sack under his arm, he carefully closed the lids.

Suddenly the sound of a rattling chain glued him to the spot. A dog's black shadow moved near the faucet beside the building. "Good dog. Good dog," he whispered.

Growling, its chain rattling behind him, the dog approached Daniel. The menacing snarl rose from deep within its throat.

"Sit. Down," Daniel ordered.

Surprised, the dog backed up and barked. Daniel did not dare to try to pass the animal. With an itchy red bump reminding him of his last tetanus shot, he did not want to get bitten again. He could only wait for the dog's next move. At that moment he heard someone running from the parking lot.

"Hey, what's going on back there?" a man called.

Daniel raced toward the fence in the direction of the picnic tables. The chain rattled behind him. As he tried to leap over the fence, he felt the dog's wet snout and a jerk at his jeans. The pickets stabbed into him as he hung suspended on the fence. The dog at his feet, the man behind him—he was caught.

The Newspaper Story

"Hey, you there!" A flashbulb flared behind Daniel. Then the man behind the camera pulled him down off the fence. "Who are you?"

"Daniel Morales."

"What do you have in that sack?"

"Food." The boy handed it over as the man drew Daniel into the light spilling from a window.

Checking the sack's contents, his nose wrinkled in disgust. "Where did you get this garbage?"

"Over there." Daniel pointed to the cans.

"What do you do with stuff like that?"

"I save it for my family to eat. Mamma's sick. The medicine costs money. There's no money left for food."

"What's wrong with your mother?" the man asked.

"She has a sick heart. She needs an operation."

"On the heart?"

"Sí, señor."

"When is she going in for surgery?"

"She does not want to go. We have no money."

"Is that so?" The man shifted his bulky camera, pulled a notebook from his suit, and started to scribble. Daniel guessed he was a member of the wedding party in the Café del Río because of his suit and the flower in his lapel. He was young and husky like a policeman. Reluctantly Daniel answered his many questions. Finally the man quit writing, put his notebook away, and aimed the camera at Daniel.

"Let me get another shot, just in case," he said. The flash blinded Daniel. Instantly he remembered the pictures of criminals he had seen in the post office. The "Wanted" posters always had two photos of the same person.

"Are you going to put me in jail?" Daniel asked.

"No. You can go home and keep the sack."

"Gracias, señor. Muchas gracias!" Daniel could have hugged the man for not arresting him. Instead, he hurried home.

Two days later Mr. Randall invited Daniel into his living room as the boy walked past his house. "Did you see the paper this morning?" he inquired.

"No, Mr. Randall. We don't take the paper."

"Do you happen to know this young feller?" The elderly man shoved the newspaper under Daniel's nose.

"It's me!" Daniel gasped. His picture stared up at him from the page. It showed him pinned to the fence, the dog at his jeans.

"Well, what do you have to say for yourself?" Mr. Randall demanded impatiently.

"I am sorry," the boy stammered.

"Why didn't you tell me that your mother is ill?"

"How—do you know she is sick?"

"The article tells all about it. Read!"

Daniel read the newspaper, then felt sick inside. The paper repeated everything he had told the man. For all to see. It was worse than being on display on a "Wanted" poster at the post office.

"I guess you don't want me to come around anymore, Mr. Randall." He did not look at his friend. His face burned with shame. Just think—he was in the paper like a criminal. People would laugh at him.

"Nonsense!" the man retorted. "If I had known about your family's struggle, I might have been able to help." He stepped to a side table and wrote a note. Sticking it and a five-dollar bill into an envelope, he sealed it and handed the letter to Daniel. "Take this to the post office for me, will you?"

"With the money in it?"

"Yes, with the money. I am asking the newspaper to start a fund for your mother's operation."

"I will post the letter." While Daniel did not understand what Mr. Randall was saying, he did grasp the fact that the old man trusted him with five dollars. Mr. Randall's faith made him feel a sense of pride. At the post office he pushed the letter into the proper slot.

The postmaster's head popped up at the window. "Aren't you the boy whose picture is in the paper?"

Daniel fought the urge to run. "Sí, señor."

"What are you doing in the post office?"

"I posted Mr. Randall's letter. He said he is asking the newspaper to start a fund for mamma's operation."

"A fund?" The postmaster seemed interested.

Seeing that the man did not appear angry, Daniel gathered a little more courage. "What is a fund, señor? Can you tell me?"

"A fund is like an account in a bank," the postmaster explained. "People contribute, and the money is used for a special purpose." The ring of a telephone suddenly called him away.

Daniel left the post office, thinking about what had happened. Mr. Randall had put five dollars into a fund for his mother. Would five dollars pay for the operation? He guessed not, for the pills had cost twice that much. Then a new thought occurred to him. Was it right to accept money one had not worked for? The question nibbled at the edge of his mind.

Out in open country the sky expanded like a blue umbrella. A pair of turkey vultures sailed high overhead. Once in a while they uttered desolate cries which made Daniel feel sad. Maybe, he thought, the vultures could not find anything to eat. Maybe they had young in the nest who could not hunt their own food.

One could feed a squirrel or a blue jay maybe, but not a vulture. Vultures were proud creatures. Instead of begging, they obtained their own food. Daniel respected them for that. Sometimes birds stole food from other creatures. Rather than letting their young die, they'd take anything they could. Stealing was not right for human beings, though.

At least the fund Mr. Randall had started was better than stealing. Rather than letting mamma die, the family must accept money from strangers. Later, perhaps, when she had gotten well, they could pay the money back. Or could they? Daniel sighed. Picking crops, they'd never make any extra money.

Then an idea cheered him for a moment. "If I get a high school diploma, perhaps I can pay the money back all by myself," he thought. Arms raised, he caught the breeze in the palms of his hands. Light and shade played across the landscape. Birds flashed overhead, sun-drenched oaks marched over the hillocks, casting shadowy pools underneath them. Golden grasses nodded in the sun, and purplish leaves rippled in the shade.

Daniel never tired of nature's many faces. He thanked God, for it was He who had designed things well. Mamma had often told him stories of how God had made the earth and how each plant and animal was His creation. The boy admired nature and often told his mother what he had seen during the day.

A horse frisked down the hillside, legs kicking, back arching. The image stayed in Daniel's mind all the way home.

As he neared the house, Linda ran to greet him. "I saw your picture in the paper, Daniel," she bubbled. "Mrs. Henderson showed it to me."

"I know. Mr. Randall showed it to me." He spotted his mother sitting on a fruit crate in the yard with Angelina on her lap. A smile erased the somberness from mamma's face.

"People brought gifts, Daniel. They say I can have my operation and get well."

"Oh, Mamma!" He buried his face in her black hair, which cascaded down her shoulders.

Linda ran into the house, returning a moment later with a plate of food. "Eat, Daniel! Taste what people have cooked for us." She pushed the plate at him. Mounds of different kinds of food covered the plate.

"Where did you get all that?" he exclaimed.

"Strangers brought the food, Daniel," his sister said, beaming happily at him. "We do not have to cook today."

Daniel began to eat. Some foods he immediately liked; others he decided he would need to get used to. Finally he scraped the last vegetable from his plate. "May God bless the kind people who cooked for us," he said, setting the plate on the ground.

"Amen," mamma responded, cuddling Angelina. Sunlight glinted in her hair. She had not sat outdoors for a long time. Her legs looked slimmer, which meant the pills were working. Interest sparkled in her eyes today. Daniel thought with horror of the days when she had lain in bed without responding to anybody. Though alive, she had seemed dead many times.

Suddenly she put a finger to her mouth. "Hush!" A squirrel sat on a branch of a nearby oak, gnawing on a nut. Ears erect, eyes alert, it watched the family in the yard.

"Look, Mamma!" Angelina clapped her hands together.

"Hush!" her mother warned too late as the squirrel leaped to a higher branch. The nut held securely in its mouth, it tapped its feet and jerked its tail.

Linda laughed. "The squirrel is angry at Angelina," she said.

"Small wonder, Linda," mamma replied. "Angelina disturbed its mealtime." She turned to the toddler. "If you want to watch animals, you must be quiet, Angelina."

Daniel leaned against the tree trunk and, peering up into the branches, wondered if he could climb up all the way. The squirrels had raised their babies high up in a nest of sticks. The young had not come out for a long time.

"Don't bother the squirrels," Señora Morales advised her son.

"No, Mamma." Daniel squatted on the ground and continued to stare up at the tree. The squirrels jealously guarded their home in the oak. Whenever strange squirrels wandered in, they chased them off. Now the larger squirrel scurried down the trunk to watch the boy with its bright black eyes. Its mate—forepaws stretched out, body flat, tail straight behind it—leaped from branch to branch. It never missed its target.

Daily the squirrels filled the yard with their noises. Intelligent creatures, they kept caches of nuts in the ground. Sometimes they forgot where they had put their food. Then they'd dig and dig, trying to find the acorns.

The younger oak popped into Daniel's mind. It had sprouted in the winter grass, far from the parent tree. Thanks to a squirrel, perhaps, it had found a choice spot. Then he thought of Mr. Randall. The old man said that thanks to education people could get good jobs.

A blue jay uttered a piercing scream. Daniel tensed, suddenly realizing what had alarmed the bird. He had paid little attention to the sound of a car driving by the front of the cabin. Now the blue car stopped. A gray-haired woman marched down the drive, a blond-haired girl excitedly hopping up and down behind her. A pink-ribboned pony tail danced on the child's shoulders. Daniel recognized the girl. She had looked at him one time from a moving car on Bertram Road. This time he knew without a doubt that the girl was smiling at him.

"Are you Mrs. Morales?" the woman addressed Daniel's mother.

"Sí, señora. Is something wrong?" Mamma let go of Angelina, and the toddler ran off into the bushes. She was afraid of strangers.

"We read about you in the paper, Mrs. Morales. So sorry about your plight. Please accept this toward your operation. Good day." The woman tossed an envelope into mamma's lap and hurried back to the car, the girl running after her. Mamma sat with a dazed look on her face.

Impatiently Linda bounced up and down, begging, "Open the envelope, Mamma!"

SHOES FOR DANIEL

"Sí, Linda." Señora Morales tore open the envelope. When a ten-dollar bill fell out, tears trickled down her cheeks. Choked with emotion, she whispered, "God bless the kind lady.'"

A little later bicycles banged against the cabin wall as three boys motioned for Daniel to come over to them. Daniel approached.

"What do you want?"

"We saw your picture in the paper. It's keen," a boy in red swim trunks explained. "Is that your mother over there?"

"Yes. Why do you ask?"

"My mom wants her to know we're donating money for the operation."

"Mine, too," a boy in faded jeans added.

"And mine is going to give blood in her name," said the third boy.

"Why don't you go and tell her?" Daniel asked.

The boys shrugged. "It makes us feel kind of crummy," the boy in the red trunks replied.

"Why are you so kind to us?" Daniel asked the boys.

"Dumb questions." The boy in the jeans picked up his bike. He mounted it and motioned for his friends to leave.

"See you around, Daniel," they said as they pedaled off.

Down the street they nearly collided with two horse-back riders. Daniel recognized the boy and the girl on the horses. They had spoken to him at the bridge about becoming a dropout. The girl reined her horse to a halt.

"We read the article about your mother," she told Daniel. "Daddy called home a while ago. He wants your mother to know that his bank started a fund for the operation."

"And my father has made one of the first deposits," the boy boasted.

"Thank you! Thank you so much!" Daniel called after the riders as they continued down the street. He felt ashamed. Once he had believed they wanted to give him a hard time.

The next day the mailman dropped off a bundle of letters. In them strangers wished mamma well. She gazed at the pretty cards, tears again spilling down her cheeks. Daniel guessed that she was happy. Some people had enclosed small checks and dollar bills. Papa put the money into a special box. Calling the doctor, he asked him to make the hospital appointment for his wife's checkup.

Contributions continued to pour in from people who wanted to give her a chance to live. Señora Morales entered the hospital, and her fund grew while the surgeons examined and studied her heart. Papa visited her after work and gave her courage. On the third day he came home after dark.

Daniel had waited up for him. "What did they find out about mamma today?" the boy inquired.

"She needs a new valve, Daniel."

"Where will they put that valve?" he asked hesitatingly.

"Right in the heart, Daniel. The doctors say mamma had rheumatic fever as a child. The fever scarred a valve. Now it is closing and cannot circulate the blood. That's the reason why she gained weight. She stores the fluids because her heart is failing."

"When—are they going to give her the new valve?"

"Tomorrow morning."

"So soon?"

"Sí, Daniel. The doctors do not want to wait.

Mamma has waited too long already. They will take her into the operating room at eight. By noon, the surgery will be over." Worry had stooped Daniel's father like a man carrying a fruit crate filled with rocks.

The boy thought a moment. "Will you see mamma before they take her to the operating room?"

"Sí, Daniel, and when she comes out, too."

"But the boss—will he fire you?"

"Not this boss. I showed him the paper, and he gave me the day off." Papa barely picked at the food people had brought to the cabin. Afterward he dropped asleep like somebody who had not slept for weeks. But Daniel could not sleep. Wide awake, he listened to his sisters' breathing. The night wind felt unusually hot. Acorns pounded against the roof, bounced off, and landed on the ground. Branches knocked together. The noises seemed to screech: "Tomorrow! Tomorrow! Tomorrow!"

Sweat trickling down his face, Daniel tossed about on the old mattress, wondering whether mamma also lay awake in her hospital bed. Was she afraid? Did she miss the family? He wished he could comfort her this special night. Finally, praying, he fell asleep.

The next thing he knew his father was shaking him awake. "Take care of your sisters, Daniel. I am leaving."

"Sí, Papa." The boy sprang out of bed. The sun was up. Without waking Linda, he nibbled on yesterday's leftovers. His sisters still slept peacefully. The walls of the cabin pressed against him. He went outside. More than anything, he needed space. Linda would hear the news of her mother's operation soon enough. As far as he was concerned, she could miss the day at the Hendersons.

Where Is Angelina?

The moon hung in the pale blue sky above the canyon like a yellow dinner plate. Soon it would slip over the hills still blushing from the early morning sun. Daniel ran his fingers over the peeling paint of a pasture fence. A small herd of brown horses clipped the tinder-dry grass. No dew showed anywhere. One horse lifted its head, neighing. Its wind-blown black mane reminded Daniel of his mother's long hair when she worked in the fields. Soon now, they'd wheel her into the operating room.

"I will go to the grandfather oak," Daniel decided. "Perhaps it can tell me how to be strong." He followed the trail to the old tree. "Can you help me, abuelito? I feel very low today. I feel like somebody who has stumbled over dirt clods with a bucket of fruit on his shoulder."

The oak braced itself on the hillside, its strong roots anchoring its massive trunk. As the boy sat silently beneath the ancient oak, it seemed as if its ageless strength flowed into him, calming him, easing his pain and worry.

"Plop, plop, plop!" Horses turned into the trail and galloped past him. Teen-age girls sat high in the saddle, their hair streaming behind them like plumes of spun gold. The girls' laughter rang out among the trees. Daniel watched until the last coppery horse vanished out of sight.

He thought of his sister Linda. One day she would be a teen-ager. She would work and take care of other women's babies. Kneeling in the dirt and harvesting crops, her face would turn leathery like his mother's, and nobody would remember that Linda was once a pretty girl. Daniel faced the oak. "You know many things, abuelito. Have you a secret to tell for my sister Linda?"

Wind sang through the tree's branches and leaves. Daniel listened to its song, unable to understand its message. Next time maybe, he thought to himself, if he paid attention very hard, he would learn the words. Dry leaves rustled under his feet as he went down the path.

Downhill, his ear caught tapping sounds. High on a telephone pole, a woodpecker hammered away. Daniel shaded his eyes to see the bird better. The woodpecker took flight—a flurry of black and white—and flew across the road.

The telephone pole bristled with holes. The boy noticed a second woodpecker on the pole's crossbar. An acorn clamped in its long beak, the bird hopped to the upright pole. It dropped the acorn into a cavity and gave it several extra pecks, making sure it stayed in place. The first woodpecker returned to drill new holes. Daniel watched the pair in admiration, thinking of the storehouse the woodpeckers had built for themselves. Come winter, their cupboard would be filled with food.

He walked home in deep thought. God gave the woodpeckers sense to save for meager times. Maybe God wanted people to save for bad times, too. He must tell his father about the woodpeckers. The news of his mother's operation had spread like the seeds of a puffball. People sent the family coins and dollar bills. Papa must save the money like precious acorns. Surely the doctors would ask pay for the good work they were doing on mamma.

Checking the cabin, Daniel found it empty. Where was Linda? Where was Angelina? He fought the fluttery sensation in his stomach.

"Linda went to work. She took Angelina with her," he explained his sister's absence to himself. For a moment he thought of checking at the Hendersons', but then decided it might not be wise. Linda was busy, running the vacuum cleaner and helping Mrs. Henderson. If he kept his sister from her work, maybe the woman would fire her. He shrugged off his uneasy feeling.

Down the street, Mr. Randall's mailbox gaped empty. The blinds frowned at the house. Daniel sighed. He would have liked to talk with his friend. As he walked on, brown leaves sailed through the air. Dust whirled in little funnels on the pavement.

Two white geese stuck their necks through a picket fence. Their white coats made him think of nurses. Would the nurses be good to his mother? And the doctors, would they hurt her? Daniel picked up a twig and offered it to the geese. They grabbed it with their orange bills and nibbled. Maybe they were hungry. Quickly he looked around. Like closed umbrellas, brown leaves dangled from a buckeye. He could see its large pear-shaped pods hanging from the branches. Jumping up, he tried to tear off a branch with some of the pods.

The branch did not break off. As he dropped back

to the ground, an old battered car careened around the bend. Springing sideways, he fell inches from the passing auto.

Pain pinned the boy to the ditch. The car slowed, and the driver looked back. For a moment Daniel hoped the man would stop, but the car disappeared around the next bend, trailing a plume of black exhaust fumes. Coughing from the smoke, he struggled out of the ditch and limped to a nearby rocky ledge. The fall had skinned his left wrist and both hands. The wrist and left leg smarted more than the hands. When the pain eased, Daniel hobbled across the street. The pavement was hot against his bare feet. He hoped the doctors kept mamma's operating room cool. The day was going to be a scorcher.

A hot gust of wind sent leaves hurtling along through the air like brown-skinned messengers. Daniel hoped his father would bring a good message from the hospital.

The blinds in Mr. Randall's window still indicated that he was asleep or not at home. The cabin the family rented was empty. Daniel could not tolerate its grave-yard stillness. His left leg still hurting him, he hobbled outside.

A drone filled the pale blue sky as several airplanes flew through the feathery clouds. One plane circled high in front of the sun, then dipped—its wings glinting in the sunlight—over the chimneys above the mercury mine.

The fire station's white barn stood empty, the fire truck gone. The station house atop the hill echoed with the mechanical voices of loudspeakers telling of forest fires in the hills. A plump fire-fighting plane flew low over the Café del Río. Seconds after it passed overhead, doors banged open, and four or five people ran outside.

"What's going on?" they asked Daniel.

"The firemen are fighting forest fires in the hills," he yelled against the wind.

"Where?" two men asked.

"Up there!" The boy pointed above the mine.

"Let's go!" The men jumped into a parked car and careened up the highway.

The plane roared back and circled over the Café del Río. Daniel shaded his eyes and watched it. He wished he could fly with the plane—wished he could help fight the fire.

"Firemen are important people," Daniel told himself. "If fires eat the crops, braceros have no work. Truckers cannot deliver. Markets cannot sell. People cannot buy fruits and vegetables." What did it take to become a fireman? His head whirred.

"But pilots are important, too," he thought. "They help the firemen." How do you become a pilot? The plane vanished over the hills, and he hobbled up the highway.

At the first cluster of houses, two mongrel dogs shot downhill toward him. With terror, Daniel recognized them as the ones who had attacked him before. The brown female who had bitten Daniel was not with them today. The woman had given her and the pups to the pound, stressing that Daniel was lucky because he needed no rabies shots. Having received enough injections already, he had been glad to escape the painful rabies series of shots. Now, not wanting to get bitten again, he ran home as quickly as his injured leg allowed.

In the kitchen, he caught his breath. A pie cheered the scarred counter. "For the Morales family on their big day," an attached note said. No signature showed who had brought the pie. At the thought that people cared, warm feelings rippled through him. Anglo people could actually be kind to a bracero family.

A carton of milk graced the refrigerator shelf. Daniel could not remember what milk tasted like. Filling his cup, he quenched his thirst, then, refreshed, he remembered the vegetable patch. Plants, too, suffered from thirst. Filling the battered old bucket, he poured water into the ditch surrounding the little garden. The plants abounded with tomatoes and peppers, but the tomatoes did not tempt him today. All of a sudden, he did not feel so well, and his stomach began to rumble. The milk seemed to rush through his body. He didn't know that many people in the world cannot drink milk. Their bodies lack a special chemical needed to digest it.

Hands pressed against his stomach, Daniel waited for Linda to come home. Finally the girl bounced around the corner, carrying a tray of brown biscuits, still warm from Mrs. Henderson's oven. At the door Linda looked around. "Where is Angelina?" she asked.

"Didn't you take her with you?" He promptly forgot his aching stomach.

"Of course not. She was sleeping when I left. Why didn't you watch over the baby?" Suddenly she burst into tears.

A vise of fear squeezed Daniel's chest. Everything seemed to be happening today—mamma's operation, the fire, Angelina missing. "Don't cry, Linda. We will find the baby before papa comes home."

"Where could she be?" his sister wailed.

"We must search, Linda. Don't worry. We will find her." He did not voice his fear that the toddler might be in real trouble. He had found that New Almaden bristled with all kinds of dangers—speeding cars, galloping horses, mean dogs, poison oak, sheer cliffs, deep spots in the creek. A little girl like Angelina was no match for such threats.

"Let's start on the hillside. Come, Linda!" Together the brother and sister combed the smoke-covered hills behind the cabin. Cupping their hands to their mouths, they called Angelina's name over and over. But the roar of the wind and airplanes drowned their yells. Finally their voices began to give out, and they still had found no trace of their sister.

"Don't cry, Linda," Daniel rasped, his throat hoarse. "We will find the baby."

They searched near the mercury mine, by the grandfather oak, under the highway bridge, along the creek, out in the valley—but with no success.

"It's no use, Daniel," Linda said at last, looking completely exhausted. "I cannot walk anymore."

He grasped her arm. "Let's go home and rest." His bones ached as if he had worked all day.

The red sun dipped over the hills. Soon their father would come home, and they would learn about their mother's condition. Daniel dared not think what would happen if they didn't find Angelina, but he couldn't think of anywhere else to look. They had searched everywhere.

Dusk veiled the canyon, and a blood-red sky glowed above the mine. Supposing, Daniel thought, the child had headed for the fire? Since Linda was upset enough already, he did not mention his fear to her.

Returning to the cabin, they searched every spot where the infant could possibly hide. Two hours passed. Then the glare of headlights swept across the yard as their father's pickup bounced into the driveway. Linda ran crying to the door.

Shoes for Daniel

"Papa, Papa!"

"Do not cry, Linda. Your mamma, she is alive!" Picking the girl up, he hugged her, tired lines etching cobwebs in his smiling face. Unable to help himself, Daniel sobbed out loud. Señor Morales tilted his son's face up toward him. "Do not cry. The operation, it was a success."

"Oh, Papa, I am not crying on account of mamma. It's Angelina—she's lost!"

13

Shoes for Daniel

"Angelina missing?" The news hit papa like a club.

"We searched everywhere," Daniel said between sobs. "We couldn't find the baby."

Señor Morales shook his son. "Did you ask people if they had seen her?"

"People? No, Papa." He had been learning so long to avoid people to keep from getting hurt by their cruelty and indifference that he had never even thought of asking others for help.

"Then let's go!" They charged out of the cabin and hurried from house to house. Nobody had seen Angelina on Main Street, and nobody had noticed her at the restaurant corner. At the house on the hilly bend, the terrier yipped to announce their arrival. Papa rapped on the screen door. When the woman answered the knock, she was not wearing her curlers this time.

"What can I do for you?" she asked.

"Have you seen a child of two and a half, señora?" Daniel's father asked. "My daughter, she is missing."

"I have indeed." The woman pulled the door ajar to reveal Angelina sitting on the floor in her panties, shaking a baby rattle.

"Look, Papa!" the child crowed with delight.

"Angelina!" Papa gathered her in his arms. Holding her tightly, he faced the woman. "Muchas gracias, señora. We are much obliged."

"Don't mention it." The woman waved off his thanks.

"Where did you find our sister?" Linda inquired. "My brother and I had searched everywhere."

"The puppy spotted her under the wash lines. The little girl must have waded through the creek. She was wet."

"And she followed you to the house?" Linda's mouth formed a surprised circle.

"Far from it!" the young woman exclaimed. "The little girl didn't crack a smile, and she didn't let me touch her. She hid behind the sheets like a frightened animal. I had to coax her to the house with the baby rattle."

Linda attempted to wrest the rattle from Angelina's tight fist. "She never had such a toy before."

"She can keep the old thing," the woman commented, holding the door open for them. The puppy dashed outside behind Daniel. "Puppy, come back!" she called. Daniel retrieved the terrier, and the woman gave her pet a little slap. "You silly pup," she scolded, banging the screen door shut. "You'll get yourself run over."

Daniel felt ashamed that he had misjudged her. She was actually kinder than he had imagined. But why did she act in such a cold way? Too tired to figure it out, he decided that all that counted was that the day had ended well. Back home, he fell into bed like a sack of beans.

During the night, odors of fire and smoke drifted into the porch where he slept. Daniel dreamed that he was a fireman, fighting a big blaze. But when he awoke, he was only the bracero's son—a nobody.

Linda clattered about the stove, the toddler at her heels. After breakfast, when Linda started to leave for her baby-sitting job, Angelina ran screaming after her. The child did not want to be left alone again. Linda led Angelina back inside. "What am I to do with her, Daniel?" the older sister asked in desperation.

"I will come along and keep her for the day," he offered. "We must be extra nice to her so she'll forget what happened yesterday."

"Gracias, Daniel." After Linda combed Angelina's unruly hair, Daniel tied the green ribbon at the neck. Stubborn ringlets escaped from the ribbon and framed the little girl's face. Linda slicked them back. After pulling the too-short, faded dress over Angelina, Linda sighed when she saw the panties showing a full two inches. "I wish I could sew, Daniel. Mrs. Henderson makes dresses on her sewing machine."

"Sí, Linda." He grasped Angelina's hand. The toddler between them, Linda and Daniel headed for the Henderson house. Sheets and pillowcases fluttered on the clothesline at the house on the hilly bend. Linda looked wistfully at them. "I wish we could stay at the cabin, Daniel."

"Why do you say that?"

"Because someday we might get sheets and pillowcases. And perhaps mamma could get a bedspread. One with flowers on it and pretty colors—pink, yellow, green."

Daniel frowned. "Where did you see a thing like that?"

"At the Hendersons'."

"The Hendersons are rich," he commented. Ever

since she started helping Mrs. Henderson, the girl had had strange ideas in her head..

"Don't you want to stay at the cabin, Daniel?" she persisted.

"Maybe."

"If you were rich, what would you wish to buy most?" Linda asked.

Daniel looked down at his feet. "Shoes."

"Oh." She fell silent.

He knew what she was thinking. "Shoes are for rich kids, not for us." She didn't say it aloud. Linda would rather bite her tongue than hurt one of the family. But her somber face spoke louder than words. Daniel studied his oldest sister. Callouses no longer covered her knees. Her hair no longer showed tangles. Her blouse and jeans were clean.

"I hope we can stay at the cabin, Linda. I may ask papa." He meant what he had said.

"Gracias, Daniel." A smile touched her eyes and set them dancing. At the Hendersons' she dashed into the house like one of the family. Daniel turned back and carried Angelina past several yapping dogs. Near the end of Bertram Road a familiar bleating coming from a porch stopped him.

Daniel rubbed his eyes. His old friend, the goat, stood on the porch steps. "How did you get up there?" he demanded. "You're supposed to live on Main Street." He had missed seeing the little goat. "Anyway, I'm glad you found a good home," he told the animal. "If I'm lucky, maybe I will get a good home, too."

Daniel had spent a whole summer away from the crops. His family had spent May, June, July, August, and part of September at New Almaden. Never before had they stayed so long in one place. He wished they could remain there, but his father was a bracero. Braceros were migratory people. They followed the crops. The boy's gaze surveyed the trees, birds, squirrels—all the world around him. He would miss the place.

New Almaden showed a hundred different faces. One by one, Daniel had discovered them. He had listened to the voice of a summer creek, had watched wild creatures, and had dreamed in the shade of trees. Yes, he would even miss the people of New Almaden—those strange people who hid their kind hearts behind a frowning shield. But *knowing* they were kind made the difference.

With Angelina trying to keep up with his steps, Daniel passed La Casa Grande. The mansion napped like a tired old lady. No music, no laughter, drifted from the backyard. The swimming pools had closed after Labor Day when New Almaden's children went back to school.

Mr. Randall's mailbox was empty, but the old man's cotton-white head showed at his living-room window. He waved at the boy, so Daniel carried his sister across the street.

He introduced his littlest sister: "This is Angelina, Mr. Randall."

"What a cutie pie!" Mr. Randall's brisk voice scared Angelina, and she pulled away.

"She is shy with strangers," her brother explained.

"How is your mother, Daniel?" the man asked.

"Thank you for asking, Mr. Randall. The operation was a success. When mamma gets well, we can move on."

"Where would you go at this time of the year?" Mr. Randall seemed upset.

"To Arizona maybe."

SHOES FOR DANIEL

"And what about next spring?"

"We'll follow the crops as always." Daniel accepted his friend's silent invitation to sit on the davenport, where he held Angelina on his knees.

Mr. Randall pulled a paperback from his bookcase. "This is for you, Daniel, for bringing the mail."

"A book?" The boy set his sister on the floor.

"A bird book," his elderly friend corrected. "You like birds, don't you?"

"Yes, Mr. Randall." Daniel studied the colored pictures. Close up, the birds looked even more beautiful than when he had seen them from a distance. Daniel recognized blue jays, mourning doves, blackbirds, finches, hummingbirds, and—"Bushtits!" he cried. "That's the name of the birds Linda showed me. You should see them, Mr. Randall. They're the tiniest, busiest birds you ever saw. They're right here in this book. They call them bushtits!"

"Bushtits catch insects in my yard." Mr. Randall smiled happily. "Do you like the bird book?"

"Yes, sir, Mr. Randall. Thank you very much." He paused a moment. "I wish I could read better, though. I would like to learn more about nature."

"They teach about nature in school, Daniel."

"I—uh, papa does not want me to go. He says school is not for us. Our people have always ·been braceros."

Mr. Randall eased himself down on the davenport and sat lost in thought. Finally, after a long silence, he replied, "You can shape your own future, Daniel. Because your father was a bracero—that is no reason you must spend your life doing the same thing. Our country holds opportunities for everybody. All you need to do is to grasp them."

Daniel hung his head. "Papa says I am not so smart. He says people like us do not learn so well."

"You must not think like that. Nobody will respect you if you don't respect yourself."

"How can I do this—respect myself?" the boy asked.

"Quit being ashamed of what you are. Count your assets. What do you have that other children lack? Explore your background. What have your people accomplished in the past? What can they do in the future? Think about such things, Daniel. It will help you."

"If I go to school, I will sit with fourth graders. I am behind for my age." He tried to digest his friend's advice.

"If you study hard, you'll catch up with the children your own age, Daniel. If you stay, I'll help you with the schoolwork. Would you like that?"

"Oh, yes, Mr. Randall!" The old man's promise filled him with hope. "Would you—talk with papa, please?"

"I might do that, Daniel," Mr. Randall answered, nodding vigorously.

Señora Morales was doing well at the hospital. Every evening Daniel's father brought home good news about her recovery. Nine days after her surgery, she came home. Though in pain, she seemed happy. She let Daniel listen to the faint click of her new heart valve and help her walk around the cabin. Her ability to walk indicated that she was healing. With the aid of skilled doctors and caring people, God had performed a miracle. Grateful, the boy no longer worried about his mother.

He did worry about Linda and himself, though.

Going back to the crops—was it not like entering a dead-end street? Linda, Angelina, and he, Daniel—did they have any kind of future to look forward to? Every day bulldozers ripped out fruit trees. Other men were paving over fertile fields with roads and houses. More and more mechanical harvesters replaced human workers. What was a bracero child to do?

Then he had another thought. True, they had not followed the crops all summer long, but the family had still eaten. Papa had managed to pay the rent. As a janitor, he could work through the winter while Daniel and Linda attended school.

"I've wasted an awful lot of time," Daniel muttered. "Maybe I could turn it into what Mr. Randall calls an asset if I went to school and learned something important."

The day after mamma came home, Daniel's father parked his pickup at Mr. Randall's house. The next day, he installed a new muffler on the truck. And a day later he washed and waxed the pickup. Daniel watched his father's activities with mixed feelings. Papa always prepared the pickup before taking off for Arizona.

"Mamma cannot travel. She is still healing," Daniel reminded him.

"I know, Daniel," his father replied, rubbing the grimy layers of dust from the hood.

"Then why do you fix the pickup?"

Papa straightened up. "Your papa, he will make important errands tomorrow."

"What kind of errands?"

"You will find out."

The following morning, papa shaved and donned a clean shirt and freshly washed pants. Bursting with curiosity, Daniel followed him to the pickup. Papa started the motor and waved back. "Until tonight, Daniel."

The gleaming pickup rolled down the drive, sunbeams bouncing off the polish. At the corner, the pickup did not roar or clatter. The muffler silenced the exhaust.

What was papa up to? Daniel wondered. Was he preparing for the winter trip? At least he had not put the pipes on the pickup bed. Maybe that was a good sign.

Daniel looked after his mother and Angelina until Linda returned. Then the walls of the cabin started to press in on him, and he felt a need to get out. The problem worrying the family had vanished, but he was still not happy.

The sycamore leaves covering the sidewalk crunched and crackled beneath his feet. Trying to cheer himself up, Daniel reminded himself that he had learned many important lessons at New Almaden. But with a sigh he realized that he had not learned enough.

Acorns fell with a steady patter on the leaf-cushioned ground beneath the grandfather oak. Daniel picked up an acorn. Plump and satin-smooth, it showed the fine grain of polished wood. The work of a master craftsman, it was indeed worthy of the grandfather oak. Throughout the hot summer the oak had existed without rain, yet it had produced a bumper acorn crop.

Daniel admired the oak and the wild creatures, and wished he had their stamina. Oaks survived the rainless summer. Saplings struggled to reach the light. Woodpeckers stored food for meager times, and squirrels defended their homes. Deer risked their lives nightly to drink from the brook.

Daniel stretched his arms to the great oak. "Life gives challenges to everybody, abuelito, and why not?

Challenges make us strong. Challenges are hurdles. One must be brave to jump over them. Papa jumped over a hurdle when he asked for jobs that he knew nothing about. I have decided that I must jump over a hurdle, too, abuelito. I must get an education."

Then sadly he dropped his arms to his sides. Papa had prepared the pickup for the trip to Arizona. Come spring, the family would stoop over the fields and harvest other people's crops. Then Daniel would have little time for school.

The boy's father came home late, a paper sack clamped under his arm. "Rolando Morales, he accomplished many things today," papa happily announced at the door. "Look what I brought for you, Linda. This box, it is for you."

"A dress, for me? Muchas gracias, Papa!" Linda squealed after opening the box.

"Sí, Linda. Try it on!" Next papa turned to Daniel. "Look what I brought for you. This box, it is for you."

"Shoes!" Daniel gasped while lifting the lid.

"Sí, Daniel. Try them on!"

Carefully Daniel wiped his feet before slipping them into the soft brown leather. The shoes caressed his feet, making him feel like a king.

"How do they fit, Daniel?" his father asked, impatient to know his reaction.

"Fine. Muchas gracias, Papa! I will take care of these shoes so they will keep on shining."

"Sí, Daniel." The father's happy laugh filled the cabin as he tapped his chest. "Rolando Morales, he paid the landlord in advance," he boasted. "The landlord, he was very pleased. He gave me a lease with option to buy the cabin."

"Buy it with what?" his wife exclaimed.

"Rolando Morales, he saw a construction boss." Papa threw out his chest. "This boss, he needs cement finishers after the rainy season. He needs men like me —men with strong backs, men who can work, who can stoop. Cement finishers make much money."

A weight dropped from Daniel. The family would stay at New Almaden. But what about school? His father had not said anything about that.

High winds shook the cabin during the night. Daniel tossed and turned on his mattress. Why had his father bought shoes? Was he saying, "You can go to school. No more embarrassment about going barefoot"? The boy did not fall asleep until morning.

Then papa shook him awake. "Get up, Daniel. You must not be late."

His son blinked. "Late for what?"

"Did I forget to tell? I saw the school boss yesterday. You are enrolled, Daniel. Do not miss the school bus."

Daniel slipped into his new shoes. "What about Linda?"

"Linda will stay with mamma. She can help the Hendersons after you get back from school."

"May Linda go to school when mamma is well?"

"Sí, Daniel," papa said as he left for work.

Daniel knew where the school bus stopped. As he climbed aboard, he felt he was now one of them, the children of New Almaden. The season's first raindrops tapped a pleasant tune on the bus roof.

A grove of walnut trees bordered the road. The winds had ripped the nuts from the branches. His face pressed against the window, Daniel stared at the old cars parked beside the orchard and the bracero boys and girls harvesting the nuts. Taking a deep breath, he could hardly believe his luck. Warm and dry, he was riding to school.

The orchard yielded to a vineyard of blue grapes clustered on the rust-colored vines. Daniel remembered his first ride through the Almaden Valley. The dead-looking vines had turned into a thing of beauty. He marveled at the change. When he first saw the bristly vines, his heart had ached. Much had happened since then, for now he was happy.

The bus slowed to a halt. A girl—her black curls flying in the wind—ran down the driveway leading from the house in the center of the vineyard. Two black dogs frisked beside her. Daniel recognized the girl as the one who had greeted him while riding her horse one day. Cheeks flushed from running, she boarded the bus.

Daniel sat back in his seat. He would study hard and catch up with his grade. Perhaps someday he would share a classroom with the girl. Then he would earn a high school diploma and get a good job. And why not? He spoke two languages, knew two ways of life. Taking the good from each, he would surely come out a winner. The shoes hugging Daniel's feet seemed to whisper, "You can do it. You can do it."